The Carbon-Neutral ADVENTURES of the Indefatigable ENVIROTEENS

First published by Allen & Unwin in 2020

Copyright © Andrew Marlton 2020

SS4C logo © School Strike 4 Climate Australia and is used by kind permission.

All rights reserved. No part of this book may be reproduced or transmitted in any form or by any means, electronic or mechanical, including photocopying, recording or by any information storage and retrieval system, without prior permission in writing from the publisher. The Australian *Copyright Act 1968* (the Act) allows a maximum of one chapter or ten per cent of this book, whichever is the greater, to be photocopied by any educational institution for its educational purposes provided that the educational institution (or body that administers it) has given a remuneration notice to the Copyright Agency (Australia) under the Act.

Allen & Unwin
83 Alexander Street
Crows Nest NSW 2065
Australia
Phone: (61 2) 8425 0100
Email: info@allenandunwin.com
Web: www.allenandunwin.com

A catalogue record for this
book is available from the
National Library of Australia

ISBN 978 1 76052 612 2

For teaching resources, explore www.allenandunwin.com/resources/for-teachers

Cover design by Liz Seymour
Cover illustration by First Dog on the Moon
Text design by First Dog on the Moon and Liz Seymour
Printed and bound in Australia in April 2023 by the Opus Group

10 9 8 7 6 5 4 3

The paper in this book is FSC® certified.
FSC® promotes environmentally responsible,
socially beneficial and economically viable
management of the world's forests.

www.firstdogonthemoon.com.au

The Carbon-Neutral ADVENTURES of the Indefatigable ENVIROTEENS

by First Dog on the Moon

ALLEN&UNWIN
SYDNEY · MELBOURNE · AUCKLAND · LONDON

Dedicated to everyone
born after 415 ppm

Contents!

Frontal Bit (You're reading it) 1

Chapter 1 - Meet the EnviroTeens! 8

Chapter 2 - One morning at EnviroTeen Headquarters 20

Chapter 4 - Oh no it's the teeny tiny microbeads! 50

Chapter 5 - The Ungulate 64

Chapter 6 - Welcome to Nifflenose Island 82

Chapter 7 - Villains! 100

Chapter 8 - A Dangerous Journey 112

Chapter 9 - Welcome to the Explainatorium 128

Chapter 10 - How to put mascara on a wobbegong 146

Chapter 11 - Beverly and the compost heap of treachery 160

Chapter 12 - An Exciting Plan 176

Chapter 13 - The mystery of the stolen stollen 190

Chapter 14 - A falling out 210

Chapter 3 - It's sort of complicated 230

Chapter 16 - Denouement on the Moon! 260

Chapter 17 - The end. Or is it?! Yes it is. 284

Endle Bit 290

Who and what is who and what in this book!

A list of some important people, machines and things you will meet in these pages

Goodies (in alphabetical order)

Albury – a penguin

Beverly – a sourdough starter and Worried Norman's friend

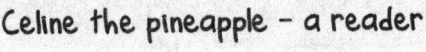
Binky – an echidna and a platypus. It's complicated but it is all explained in Chapter 3. Or is it?!

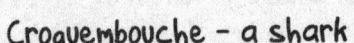
Captain Snoothole – coordinates the Nifflenose Island Sea Creature Refuge Collective

Celine the pineapple – a reader

Croquembouche – a shark

First Dog on the Moon

Letitia – a wombat (genius)

Melissa the Prime Minister's giant anteater

Mr Flooby the ESL teacher (no pic)

 Nurse Barnevelder – a chicken of all trades

Stuart – a wobbegong

 Tanya – a tiny turtle

The bandicoots – they run the workshop where Letitia and the other EnviroTeens build things

The climate change awareness pomeranians

The mysterious person who lives in the haunted volcano

Worried Norman – a young fellow who becomes Pastry person! A baked goods based superhero

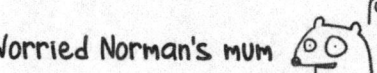 Worried Norman's mum

 Worried Norman's dad

Baddies

The microbeads – a bunch of microbeads – creepy

Singleuse Plastic Brendan – a villainous plastic bag

Mr and Mrs Thermomix – awful people

Commander Sockweasel – a wretched fellow

Free Market Phillip – disgraceful person

Professor Flappytinkle – just horrid

Colonel Clothespeg – seriously not this guy!

Mega-Patricia the Giant Carnivorous Robot – she is the worst

The Anthropegenets (bad cats) – boooo

Coal Man – an absolute scoundrel

Microscopic Coffee Carol – not Carol not now not ever!

Senior Sergeant Bellybuttonlindt – blergh gross

The sinister and mysterious BIG ROSTI Oh no!

Machines

Defoofiliser – a machine to remove excess (poison) foof from the atmosphere

Denise – a mech

 Clingwrapifier – clingwraps your face don't point it at your head

Deshellifier – turns turtles into things that are not turtles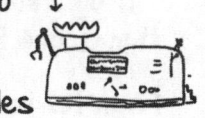

← Turtle Re-Habilitron – fixes turtles

Turtelepooter – moves turtles around against their will

EnviroHonk – the EnviroTeens' biodiesel solar-powered hoverrocket

← Space Potato – a spaceship (looks like a potato)

Hot chip outer space death ray – fries things from space

Also there is a shark who rides a scooter

 A remote control (various functions)

The Nemesispotter – villain-finding device

Scientific Disclaimer

This is a book about a lot of things and one of those things is Science. There is a fair bit of science in here, some of it is made-up and some of it is real. You will have to decide which are the true bits and which bits are less true.

Remember though, just because YOU decide something is true or not doesn't actually make it true or not. Only science can do that. If you're not sure you might look it up (I did). It is pretty easy though the made-up things are RIDICULOUS (the armpits are real though).

I can tell you in Chapter 9 the science is pretty much all true - except the bit about the world's strongest meringue. Also I don't think anyone has come from Mars yet or built an interstellar space cannon out of an old aluminium smelter and some sticks.

ALTHOUGH YOU NEVER KNOW IT COULD BE A REALLY TRULY FACT!

It isn't.

BUT IT COULD BE.

It's not though.

ONLY TIME WILL TELL!

Stop this.

* I'm not allowed to say I am a scientist because I am not one

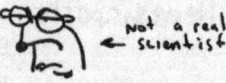

Editorial Disclaimer

Hi I'm Nicola and I am the editor of this book and I just want to say that First Dog was extremely unhelpful when I tried to fix all the punctuation in the book especially things like run on sentences which is where a sentence just goes on and on and on and doesn't have a comma anywhere to give your brain a rest even a bit. First Dog doesn't like commas and kept on saying no. Every time I suggested something First Dog would just keep shouting MORE EXCLAMATION MARKS!! So if there is anything in this book that doesn't make sense it is not my fault I tried to fix it but I wasn't allowed to and I didn't even write THIS sentence because it is a terrible sentence that just keeps going and going also I have a face like a squished tomato!!

← NICOLA

Editorial Disclaimer Disclaimer — I didn't write that first disclaimer but the part about not being allowed to edit anything properly is true it is not my fault. MORE EXCLAMATION MARKS! I HAVE A FACE LIKE A SQUISHED TOMATO!!

MEET THE ENVIROTEENS

CHIRP (NOT AN ENVIROTEEN JUST A BIRD)

CHAPTER 1 (one)

In which we travel to the Great Pacific Garbage Patch, encounter a dreadful villain and Binky gets foozed right in the face by a clingwrapifier.

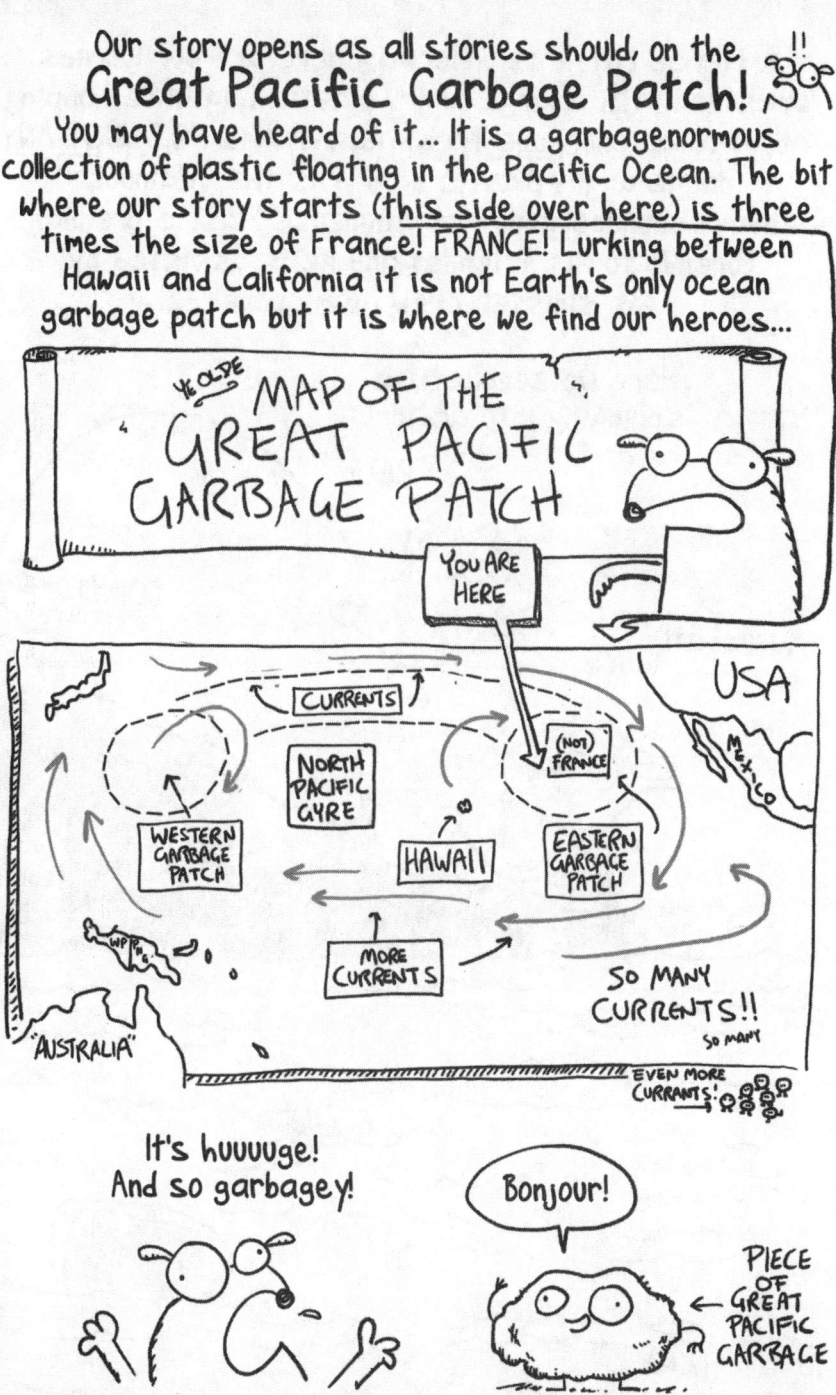

A fierce battle is underway! Here are our heroes wrestling with a large angry plastic bag while hopping about on an enormous trash island! It is NOT JUST ANY large angry plastic bag, it is the villainous enviroscoundrel known as Singleuse Plastic Brendan (Brendo to his friends) and he is assisted by his sinister crew of microbeads!

Let's take a *Science Moment!*

Did you know, the real truth about this Great Pacific Garbage Patch business is... (according to garbage patch scientists – here is one now...)

GARBAGE PATCH SCIENTIST →

← SPECIMEN NET

SPECIMEN

It contains 1.8 trillion bits of plastic! 4 pieces of plastic every square metre so it's NOT an island and you CAN'T stand on it! You CAN'T see it from SPACE – it's just water with plastic in it like a RUBBER DUCK in a BATHTUB. 4 rubber ducks in a bathtub – but TRILLIONS of them. A huge bunch of the plastic that ends up in the ocean floats to this one spot and thus ruins it for anyone needing ocean without plastic in it which to be fair is pretty much everyone – so now you know.

GARBAGE PATCH FACTS!
- Can't see it from space
- Can't run around on it
- Bigger than France! (x3)
- Has other garbage patch friends

Plastic can last for hundreds and hundreds of years. Even most "biodegradable" plastic breaks down into just MORE TINY PLASTIC. Boooooooo!

What does this mean? It means that this excellent superfight to save the turtles should actually look like this picture here

Everyone should just be SNORKERLLING ABOUT (except Binky because platypii can swim)*

WATER BALLOON

YET IT DOES NOT LOOK LIKE THIS?! Why are these pictures LYING TO YOU?! LYING! WHY?!

 LIES!

 LYING!?!

*(Two words I made up here – "snorkerlling" is NOT A WORD, "platypii" IS A WORD but is wrong)

I'll tell you why it is lying. It is lying because you are more likely to ENJOY the story if the EnviroTeens are fighting a weirdy plastic bag on GARBAGE ISLAND rather than paddling about with snorkels like a bunch of snorkel babies.

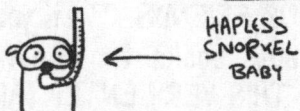

HAPLESS SNORKEL BABY

It would also be more interesting if we added **MORE SHARKS!!**

or some sharp-teethed monstrous GIGANTIC DEATH FISH THE SIZE OF A SMALLISH WHALE!!

isn't that just a big shark?

SHHHHH

You see....

BETTER FIGHTS WITH SHARKS mean YOU will ENJOY this book MORE. And the MORE you enjoy it the more you will... TELL YOUR FRIENDS. Then your friends will make whoever buys books for them go out and BUY MANY COPIES OF THIS VERY ENTERTAINING BOOK! Or why not get that person's credit card if they have one and buy them yourselves! DO IT! (no! don't do this I'm serious don't do this it was a joke not even a funny one you will get me in a lot of trouble.)

me rolling around in a big pile of author money*

* not a real picture

Meanwhile...

This is going very well.

EnviroTeen Headquarters

oof, look it's

How did we get here? — CONFUSED PICKLE

Chapter 2

In which we go back in time (a week or so) to find out why the EnviroTeens are fighting on the garbage patch. We also meet Tanya (a tiny turtle) and we are amazed by an astoundingly alliterative explanation of an unspeakable apparatus.

What?

CHAPTER TWO (2)

It's also a community centre and local arts hub and the whole thing is housed in an old artichoke canning factory so they might have found it by looking up the address on moopitymoopmaps.com.

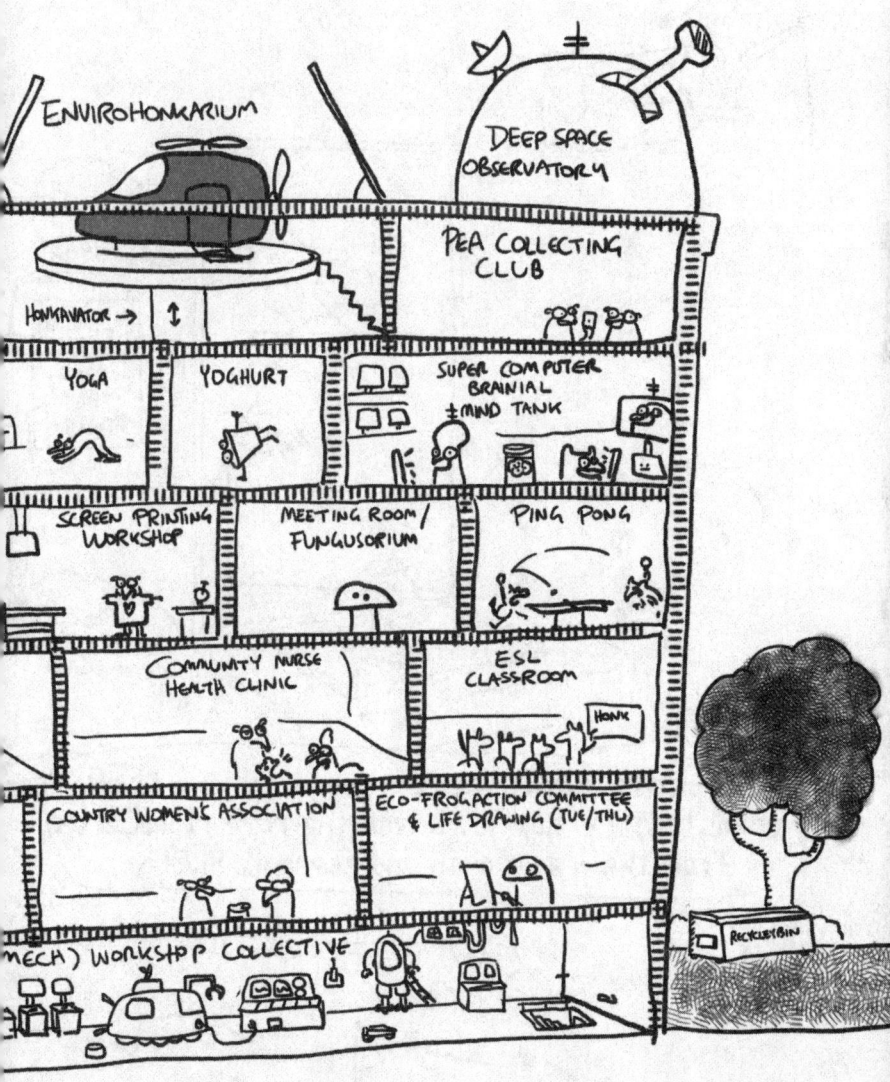

It's a tiny turtle and it has fainted!

Binky hits the "tiny turtle in trouble" alarm.

BLLAAAARTYWOOO

Everyone hurries to help the tiny turtle (her name is Tanya)

Nurse Barnevelder (the EnviroTeens' photocopier-mechanic, pilot and street medic) rushes the tiny turtle into the Turtle-Re-Habilitron.

Thank goodness we cleared your collection of toast-themed wallpaper out of the turtle re-habilitation unit on the weekend...

Let that be a lesson to all of us

I know right?!

After some turtle repair juice, a footrub and a strawberry, Tanya recovers enough to tell the EnviroTeens about the return of their old foe Singleuse Brendan the Angry Plastic Bag. Norman is shocked.

NOT SINGLEUSE PLASTIC BRENDAN?!

Yes it's him along with his awful crew of teeny tiny microbeads

NOT THE AWFUL CREW OF TEENY TINY MICROBEADS!!

Yes the microbeads and he is turtlenapping all the world's turtles

NOT TURTLENAPPING ALL THE WORLD'S TURTLES!!!

NORMAN WOULD YOU PLEASE STOP DOING THAT?!

sorry

You see Singleuse Brendan uses the telescopic turtle tracker aboard his automated battle satellite to telemetrically target a turtle for tur-tele-pooting. Then he fires a powerful projectile from the atomic turtle puncher which propels the target turtle so hard the turtle hurtles through the turtle portal and is telepooted out the aperture above the Pacific Garbage Patch and into the deshellifier.

SPACE

EARTH

← TARGET TURTLE IN OCEAN

1. Automated battle satellite
2. Telescopic turtle tracker
3. Atomic turtle puncher
4. Powerful projectile
5. Target turtle

6. Turtle hurtle trajectory
7. Telepooter ingress aperture
8. Telepooter egress aperture
9. Pacific Garbage Patch
10. Evil deshellifier

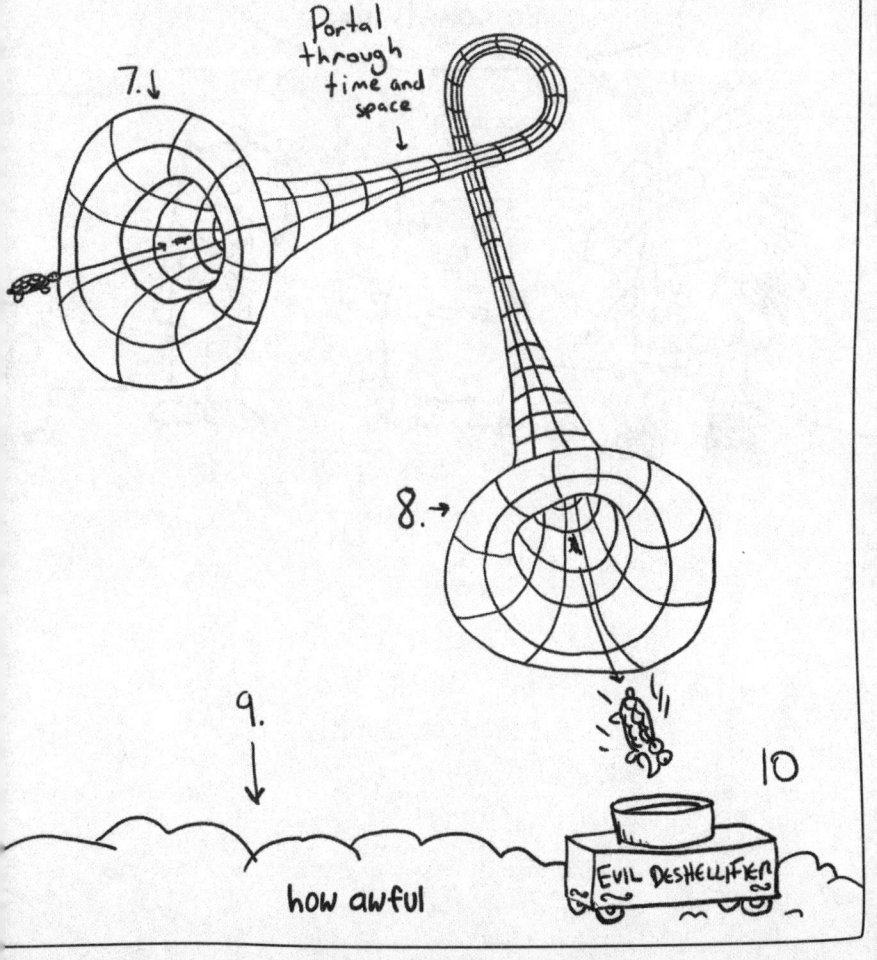

And so they did...

Nurse Barnevelder honked the
EnviroTeens signal alarm bell honker

ANYWAY

The EnviroTeens will RESCUE ALL THE TURTLES and put an end to this Plastic Brendan person and his nefarious carrying on!

OR WILL THEY?! I DON'T KNOW!

It is so exciting I can't stand it!

ENVIROTEENS CHANGE INTO YOUR VILLAIN BIFFING OUTFITS!

We really need a better catchphrase

Chapter 3 – The fight on the garbage patch!

In which...
No it can't be Chapter 3
yet I haven't changed
into my super outfit!

Come on you can do it – on the way there

No I hate getting changed in
the hoverrocket I get wrinkles
in my super tights

stares in
impatient wombat

wrinkles...

ok fine go and change
hurry up please

you too Binky

When she isn't THE MONOTREME

Binky also has a FaceTuba channel with millions of subscribers where she talks two of her favourite things, fashion and fast food.

Today's fast food is this delicious family-size ant and anchovy pizza from Aunty Gwyneth's 24hr Drive-Through Pizza Shed! It is wearing a bias cut drop waisted paisley print smock with a sweetheart neckline and taffeta ruching from the House of Crinkly and Spinkly and also some spandex leggings I found at the op shop.

I'm giving the whole outfit 6 flippers!

FaceTuba

One time during a school trip to a French nuclear patisserie, Worried Norman was bitten by a radioactive croissant. Now he can summon the power of small cakes and other baked goods when he transforms into...

PASTRY PERSON!

Just the smell of a croissant (freshly baked preferably) gives him the strength of 1000 baps!

The brain power of a gazillion muffins (American)

The tactical nous of a garden shed stuffed with baguettes. He is

PASTRY PERSON

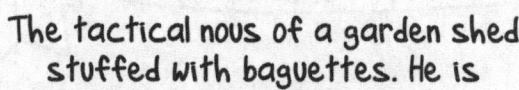

And... of course the third EnviroTeen is...

Letitia who right now is busy playing MOONMECH INCURSION on her phone — pew pew pew

Letitia's superpower is mainly being Letitia. Also she is a super inventor. And a bit bossy.

EXCUSE ME LETITIA!

What? Oh sorry yeah Singleuse Brendan! We gotta go save the turtles...

Come on people get in the EnviroHonk

It's alright for you — you don't even have to get ready

HAS ANYONE SEEN MY CROISSANT!?

It was right here...

Wait here it is!

IT'S OK I FOUND IT!!

Letitia's favourite and most gigantibrainious invention is Denise, her biodiesel-powered mech.

Sometimes it is really helpful to have a gigantic robot you can pilot around the place especially if you are just a regular-sized wombat.

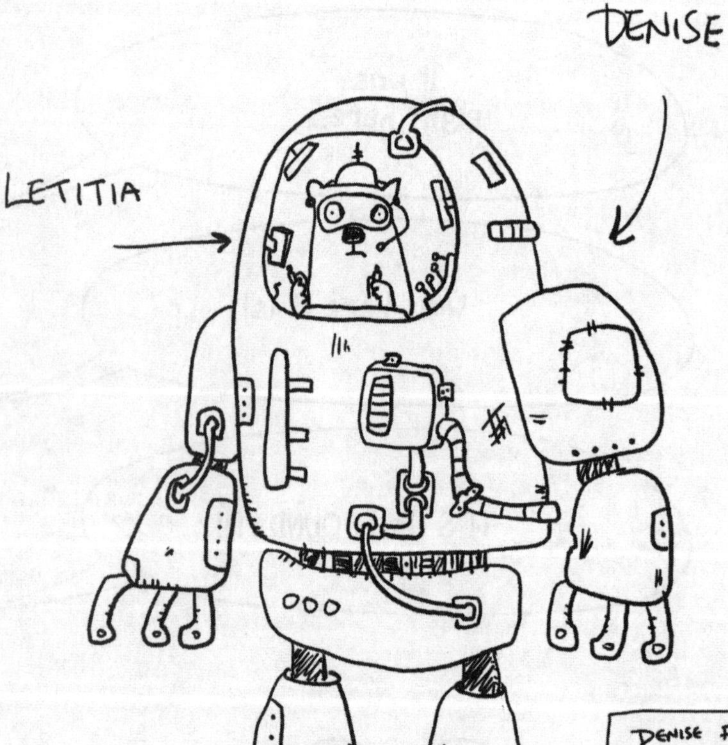

LETITIA →

DENISE ↓

DENISE FOLDS UP NEATLY TO FIT IN THE ENVIROHOME'S OVERHEAD LUGGAGE COMPARTMENT

This is Nurse Barnevelder who is a pilot, marine biologist, street medic and kazoo virtuoso. Barnevelder is the EnviroTeens' mentor and general support chicken. She flies the EnviroTeens' hoverrocket the EnviroHonk, fills out grant applications and pushes important buttons.

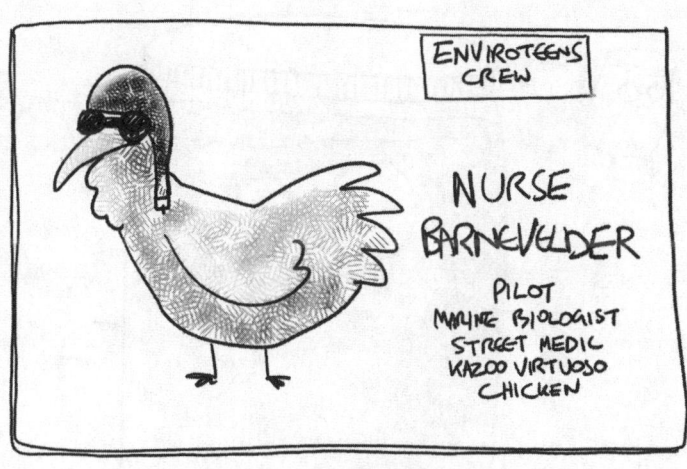

And don't forget

BEVERLY

A Sourdough Starter

Pastry Person's no-nonsense sidekick, the fierce and fabulous Beverly.

Binky's friend

STUART THE WOBBEGONG

Stuart works as second assistant director on Binky's internet video show. Stuart used to live in the aquarium but doesn't live there now.

Likes	Dislikes	Favourite food
Walking in the rain	Negative people	Fish lasagna 
Kittens	Sawdust	
Pétanque	Nets	

But who ARE the EnviroTeens?

The EnviroTeens formed when the local council funded a program to get young people interested in the community garden and destroying capitalism. They are supported by an ongoing grant from the local council who also run the community centre.

MAYOR OF LOCAL SHIRE COUNCIL

MAYOR WALLABY (DOES NOT APPEAR IN THIS BOOK)

Chapter err... 4? Yes 4!
In which we meet an enormous
plastic ungulate and Pastry
Person's feelings get hurt

NOT THE TERRIBLE TEENY TINY MICROBEADS?!

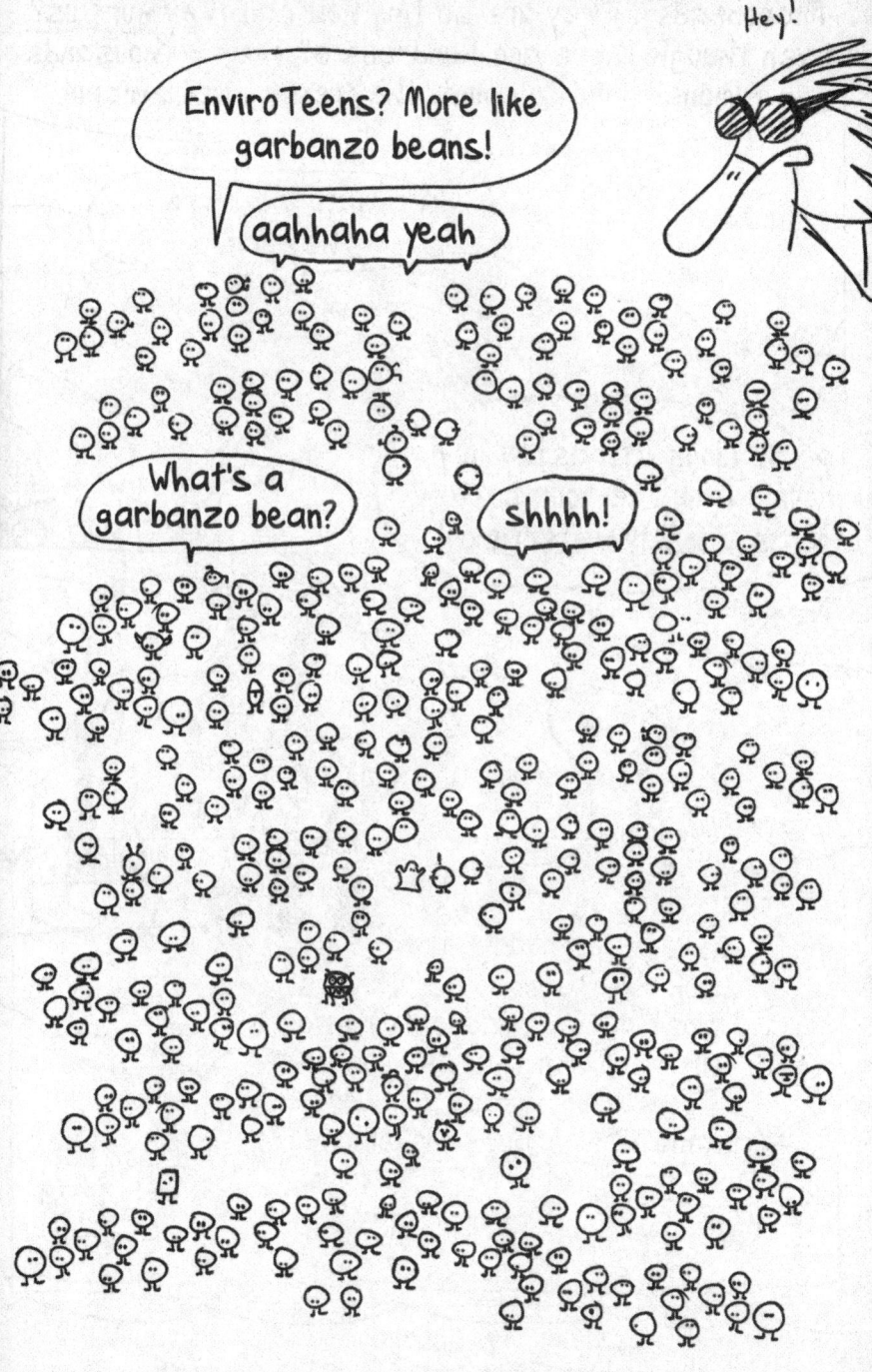

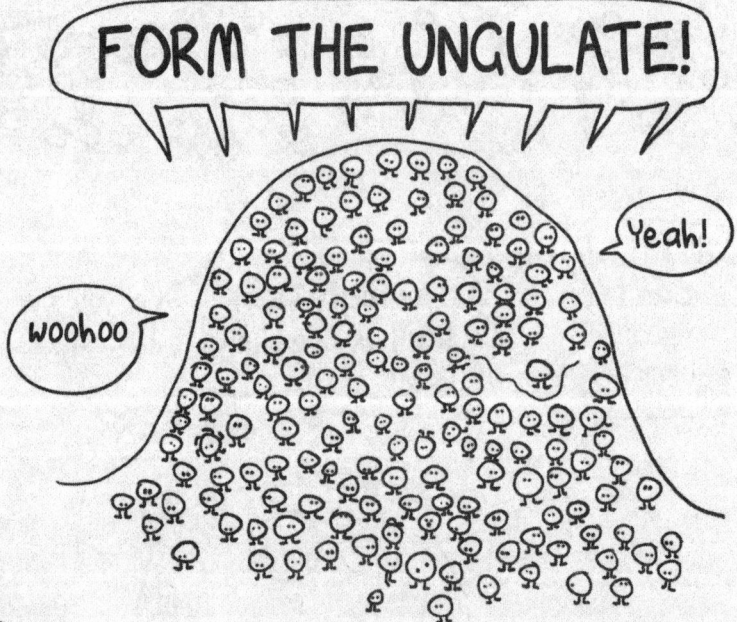

Science Moment

What even are microbeads (aside from being rude and mean)? Yes they have dreadful manners but that's not why microbeads have been banned by many (but not all) governments around the world ALTHOUGH IT SHOULD BE. You see they are so teeny tiny they get out of the toothpaste and face wash they are in and into the environment and then into EVERYTHING. Scientists are finding them in fish and drinking water and pretty much anything you can get a tiny tiny bead in - gross! We don't even understand yet the effect billionty billions of plastic microbeads will have on the environment (like SO MANY things humans do) but we just do it anyway.

Microbeads found in:

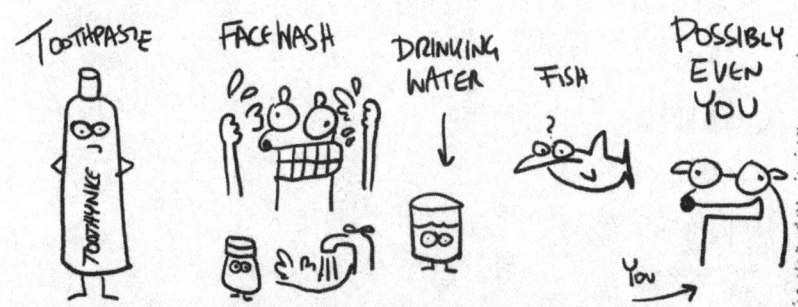

Chapter 5

THE UNGULATE

In which Pastry Person sort of saves the day accidentally unless you are a baby turtle in which case well it's sort of complicated.

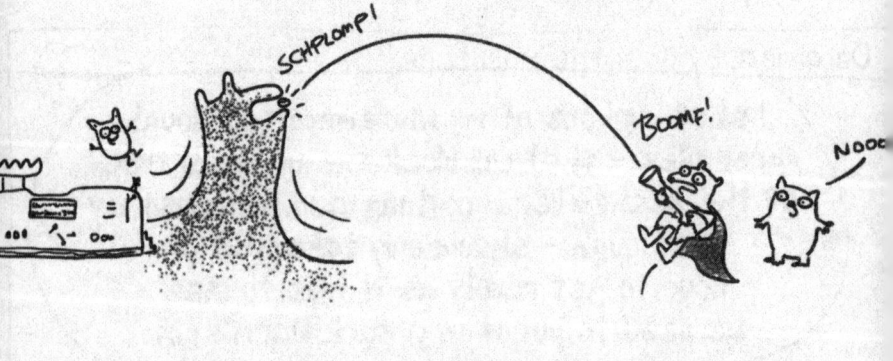

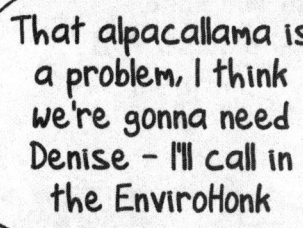

> Nurse Barnevelder would you mind dropping by with Denise please

> No problem, on my way

Seconds later the EnviroHonk swoops in towing everyone's favourite enormous mech – and drops it delicately right in front of Letitia.

Letitia leaps into the cockpit, fires up the biodiesel fusion drive and races off to confront the giant plastic alpaca.

Get that alpaca Denise!

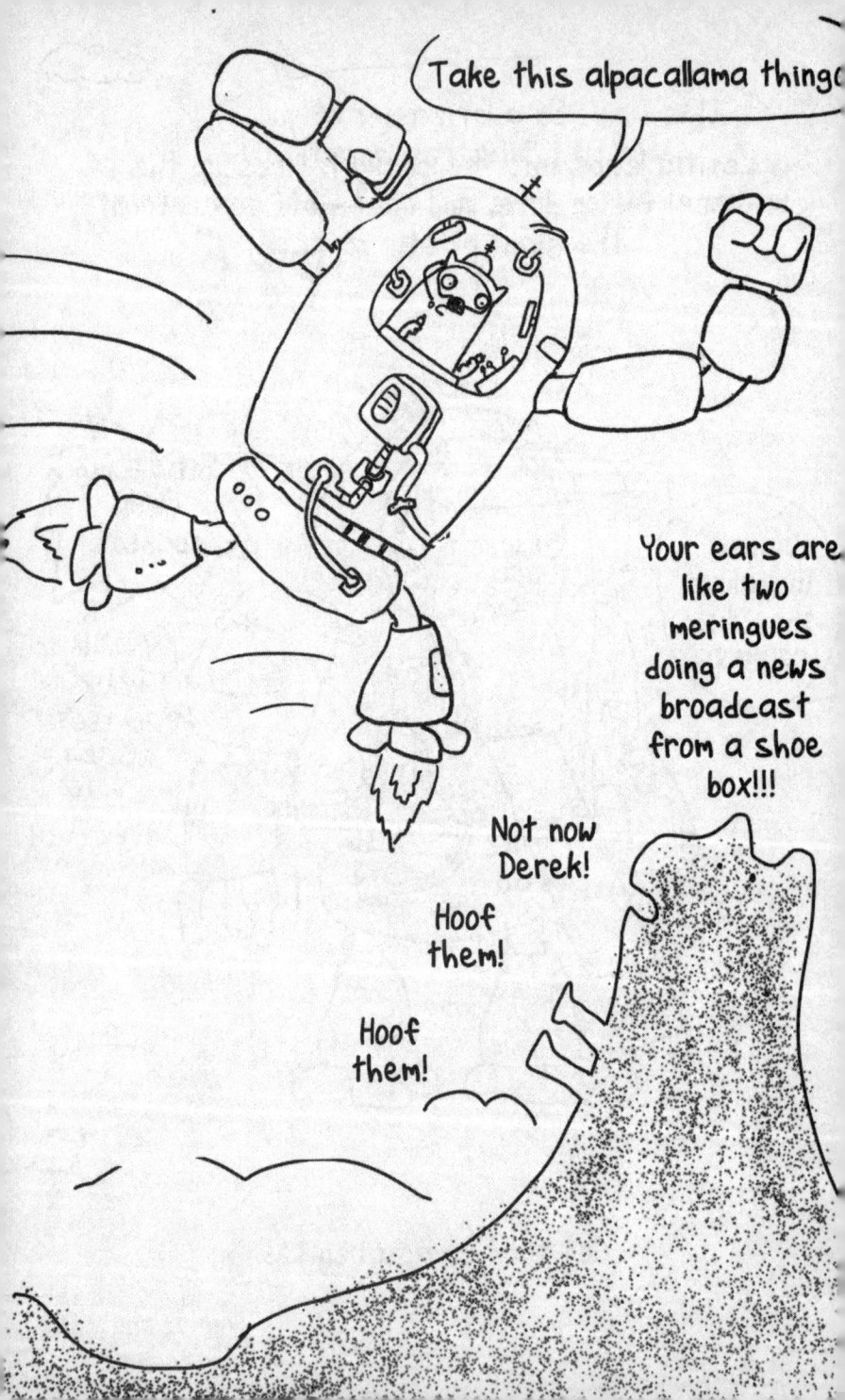

Too late! Singleuse Brendan has been turned into an attractive retro kitsch butter dish by his own dastardly machine. Oh the irony!

This is humiliating! My life's evil work destroyed!

No! Repurposing is all the rage - you're very chic

Chic!

Well... even if I am an adorable small dish, you'll never take me alive EnviroTeens!

Microbeads! To me!

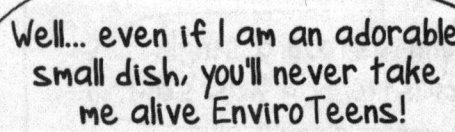

We ride!

He

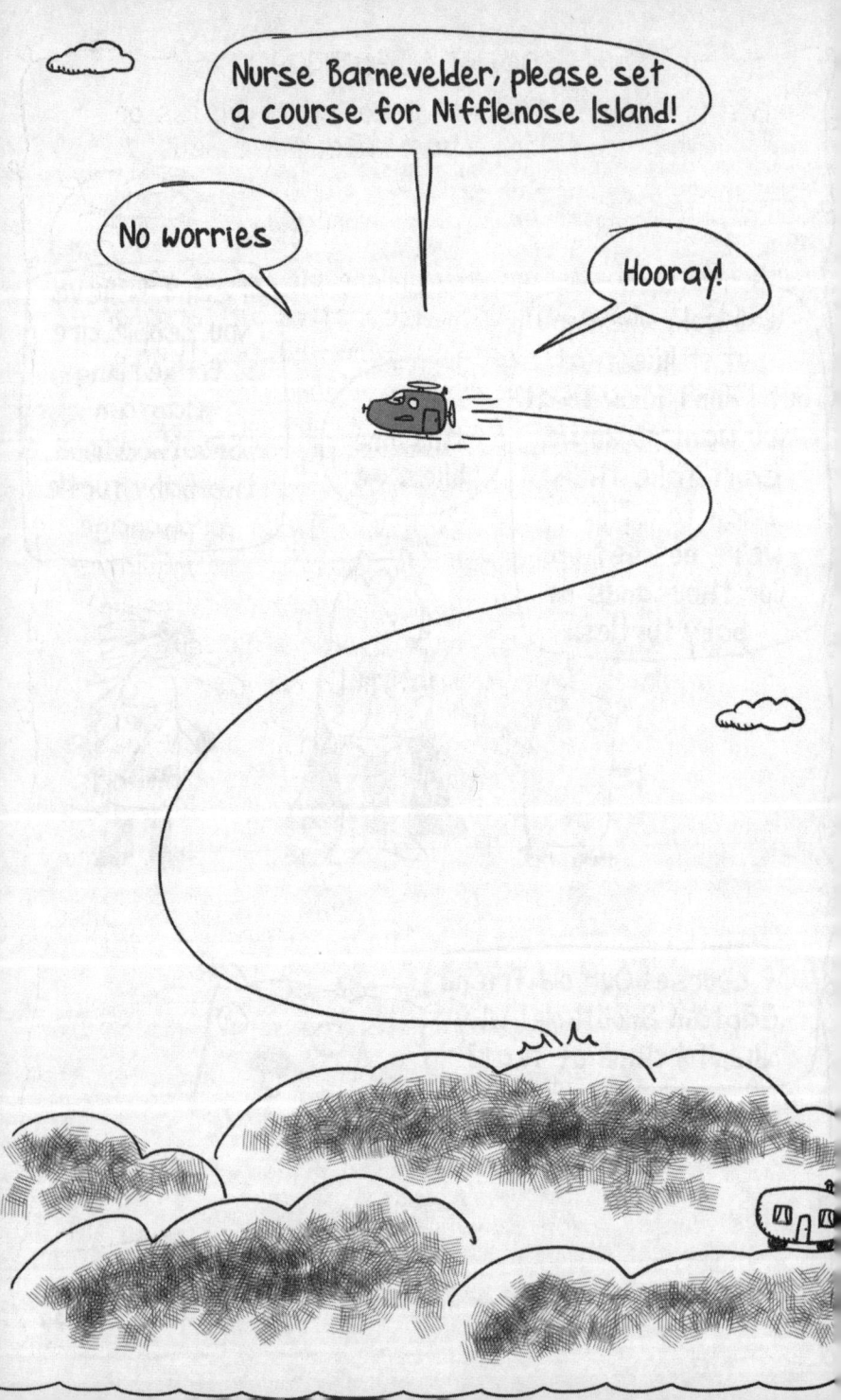

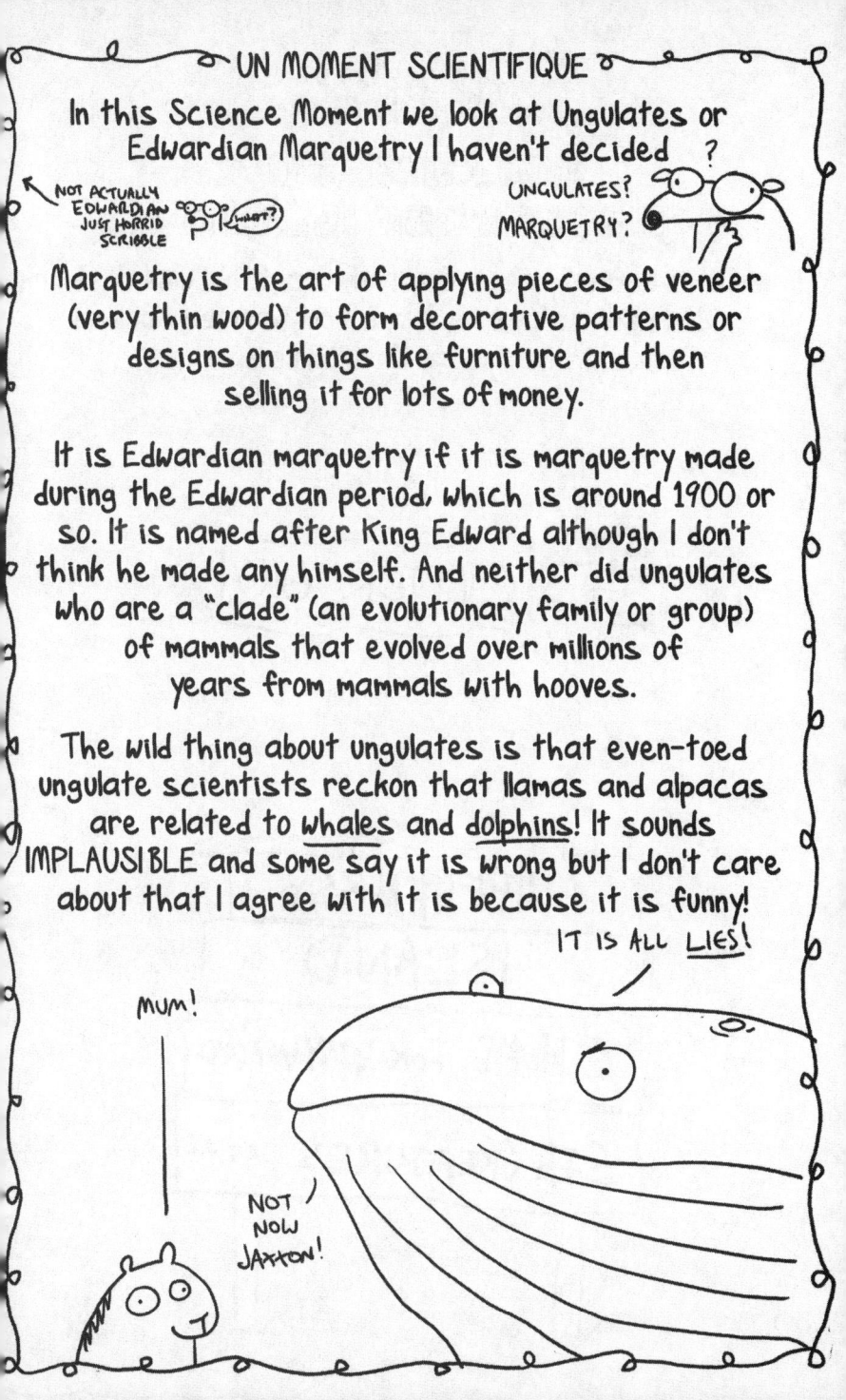

Chapter Six

WELCOME TO NIFFLENOSE ISLAND

In which we finally meet Captain Snoothole and a shark and a penguin and we learn how Worried Norman became an EnviroTeen.

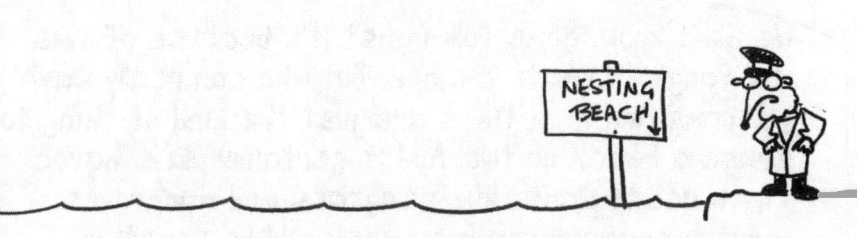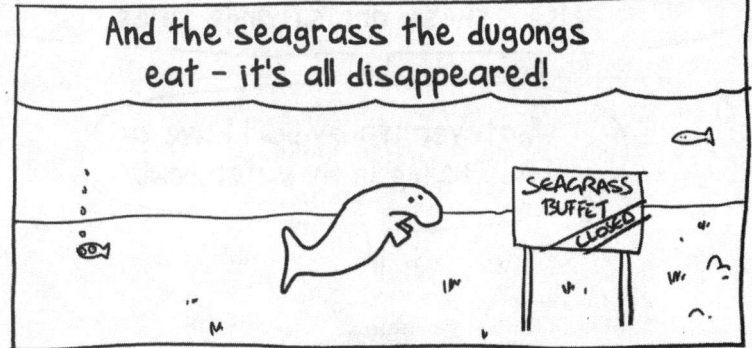

I was lonely and weird and just wanted to make friends

And I thought it sounded fun — and like I'd get to cuddle a wallaby or something

PUT ME DOWN!

Don't make it weird man

"We will have to figure it out. This may take some time."

WORD CORNER

What is a nemesis? It is a longstanding rival or an archenemy – it is that someone who always seems to turn up and cause you trouble at the wrong time – you're only supposed to have one but the EnviroTeens have loads of neminomisisses!! oh my goodness

Chapter 7

In which we find out whom is doing climate change! Or do we??! And will the EnviroTeens have to go on a spooky journey? Probably

So who is responsible for climate change? It could be ANYONE!

hmmm yes... anyone...

or it could be....

SOMEONE ELSE!

NOT THEM AS WELL?! those scoundrels!

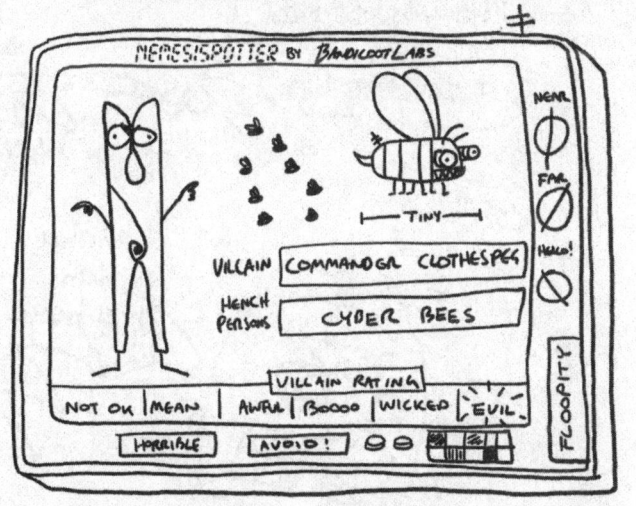

What if it is Mega-Patricia the gigantic carnivorous space robot using her massive interplanetary de-rainer to cause a global drought because she hates vegetables...

ahahah remember we blew up her rocket-powered interstellar space stationarium with that radish powered anti-matter gun? And her squadron of bullet-proof mango drones accidentally flew into the sun

She was so mad

It could be her

"Might it be that tiny but extremely wicked crew of smallish cats from Tanzania who want to sell reverse umbrellas to everyone? The Anthropogenets!"

"Those mean little jerks! What a scam. Do you think they rebuilt their radioactive umbrella factory after we buried it in the custard mines?"

I bet they did!

"Focus people focus! This isn't helping"

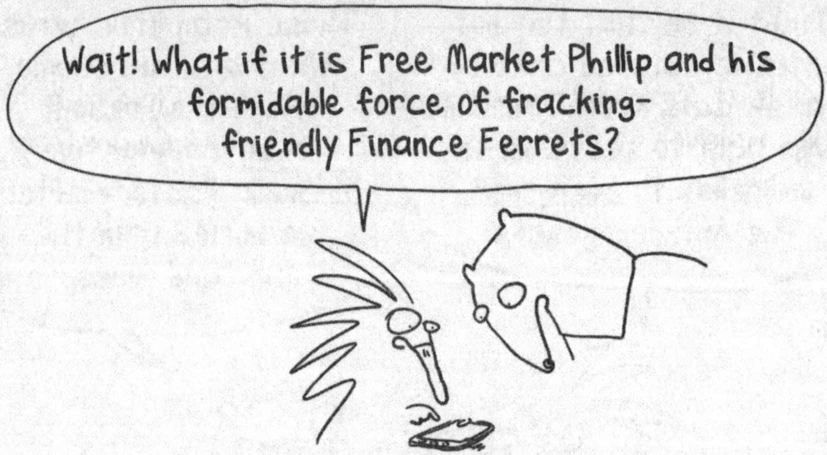

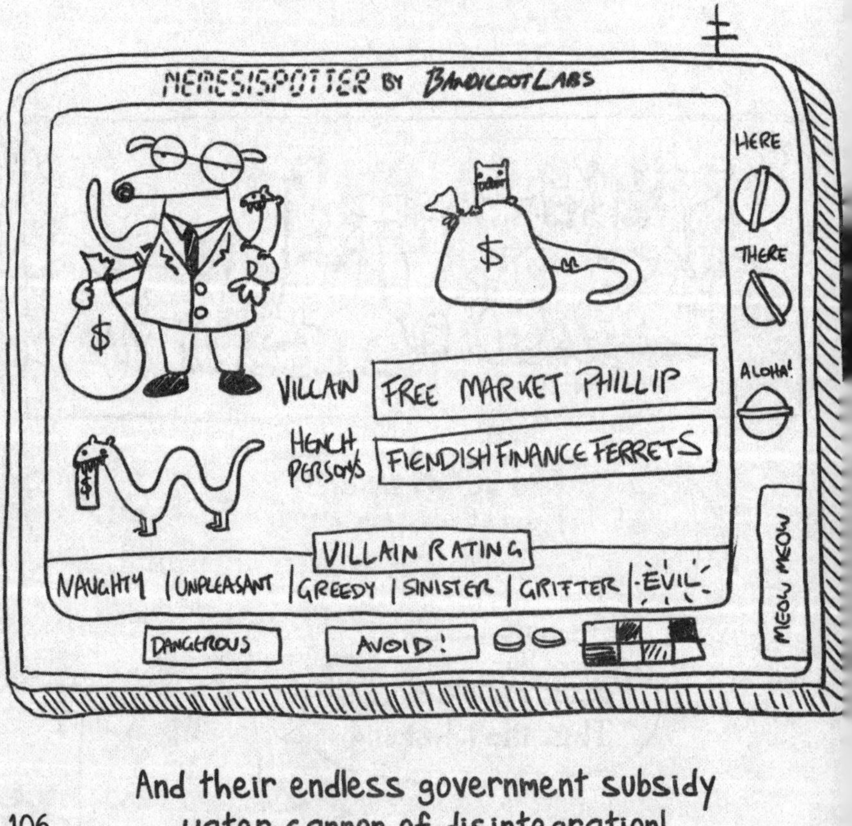

Oh no! Not Clive!

Could it be Coal Man and his inexplicable legion of unpaid internet fossiltrolls?

Or Microscopic Coffee Carol and her tiny smug army of ameobaristas?

I wonder if it is Senior Sergeant Bellybuttonlindt and the Bad Apple Gang?

I know! It's got to be Commander Sockweasel and his supersonic bison!! (bison not pictured)

COMMANDER SOCKWEASEL

There is a very wise but also mysterious soul whom knows many things — she lives in the middle of the island. Few have ever seen her but when we do she is full of good advice also really great at dinner parties.

Perhaps it is time for you to seek an audience with...

The GREAT NIFFLE!

The Great Niffle! The Great Niffle!!

the great niffle!

Is this Chapter 8?

And it's called
THE HAUNTED VOLCANO?!
Sounds a bit scary! I'M FRIGHTENED!!
IS IT FULL OF GHOSTS? AND LAVA?!

IS IT GHOST LAVA?!

Oh dear – I don't think I like this
book anymore at all

Chapter Eight

THE HAUNTED VOLCANO

In which we meet the Great Niffle and
have a tea party! With friands!
Also there is no such thing
as ghost lava. OR IS THERE?
No there isn't.

Then you have to hippity and also hoppity over the sulphurous lava ponds (they are hot AND stinky) — I hope you will not have to face the lava ghosts!

A SLOW LORIS SCIENCE MOMENT!

Slow lorises are a kind of strepsirrhine – a particular kind of monkey. They are amazing. They are extremely cute but they also have poisonous armpits and what they do is lick their armpits and then bite you and you can get sick and even die!

SLOW LORIS

POISONOUS ARMPIT(2)

POISONOUS ARMPIT(1)

TAIL

It sounds completely made-up but it is TRUE! Imagine having poisonous armpits. Go on IMAGINE IT!

Like many creatures, slow lorises are endangered – and people are mean to them by destroying their habitat, making them into pets or "medicine". If you give them a choice they live in the jungles of South East Asia where they eat fruit and smaller animals and wander around licking their armpits when they get frightened.

After the forest you must fling yourselves as flingilly as you can off the melancholy cliffs of despair and land just so in order to pass right through the mysterious purple waterfall and into the secret passage behind it — then crawl along the dark uncomfortable tunnel full of unknown WIGGLY THINGS

"Wiggly things?!"

"hmmmm maybe more squirmy than wiggly"

PURPLE ←

And last of all, you finally climb the slick and icy climb to the precipitous crumbling top of the haunted volcano and there...

And finally – if you are courageous, pure of heart and truly indefatigable – you will be ushered into the presence of the Great Niffle!

"Did somebody say friands?"

"I'll put the kettle on!"

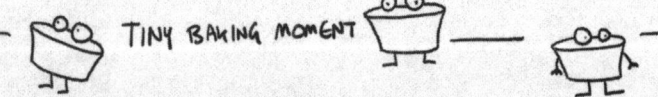 TINY BAKING MOMENT

A friand is a small almond cake, popular in Australia and New Zealand. It is closely related to the French financier, which is also a small almond cake, flavoured with beurre noisette – a type of sauce made from browning unsalted butter in a pan.

CHAPTER nine (9)
THE EXPLAINATORIUM

But what actually IS climate change?

Good news! All you have to do is put this tiny chapter into your brain via your various face holes (not up your nose! and don't eat it! - eyes or ears only please) and then you will know more about climate change than quite a few adults! True story!

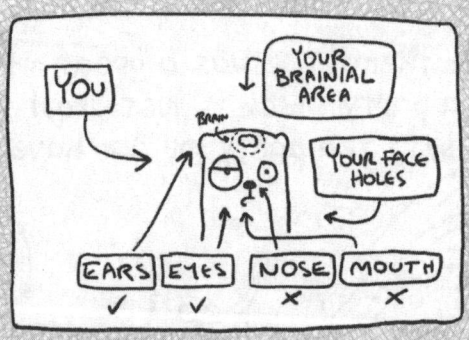

The information in this chapter is based on the science and is as true as we know.

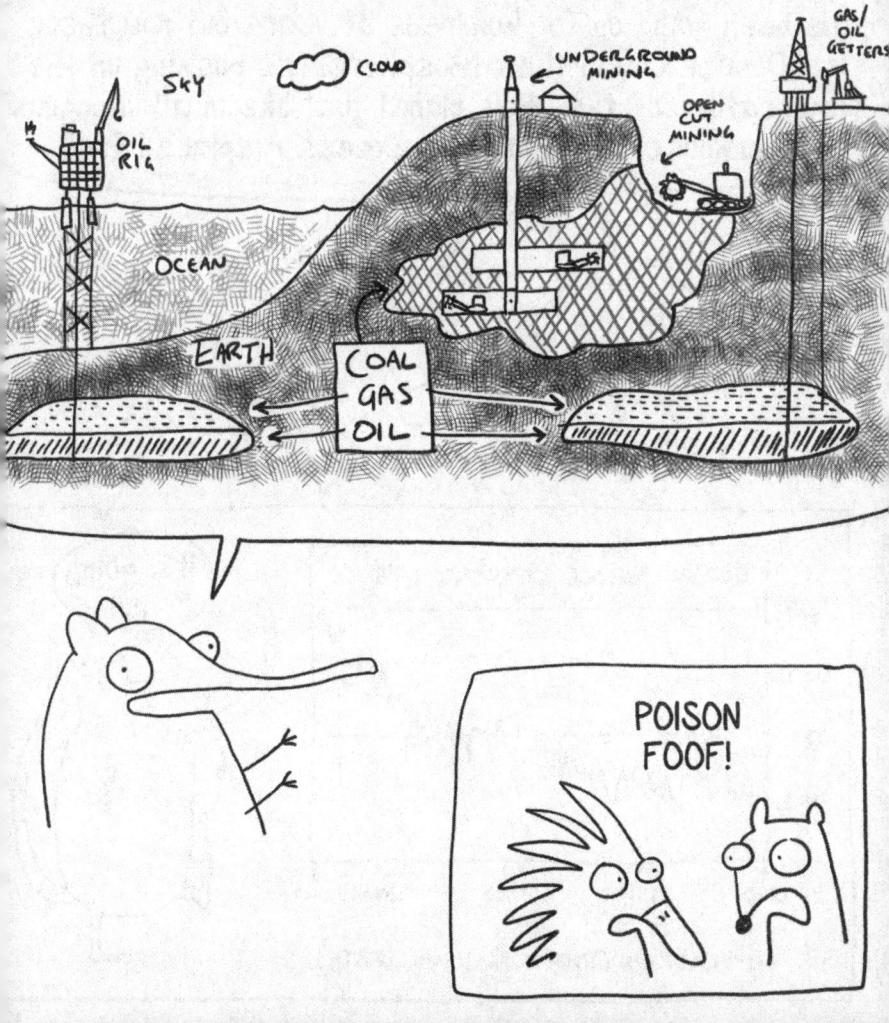

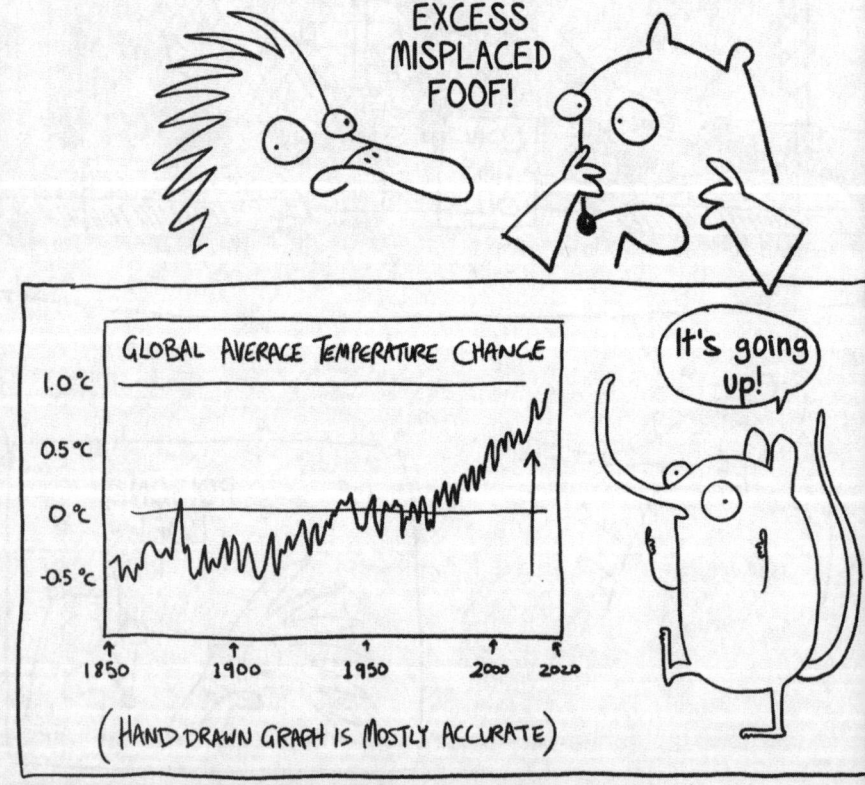

The atmosphere acts like a big blanket and that is why it is also sometimes called "global warming". CO_2 and other "greenhouse gases" like methane and their friends warm up the whole atmosphere of the Earth and it changes the entire climate.

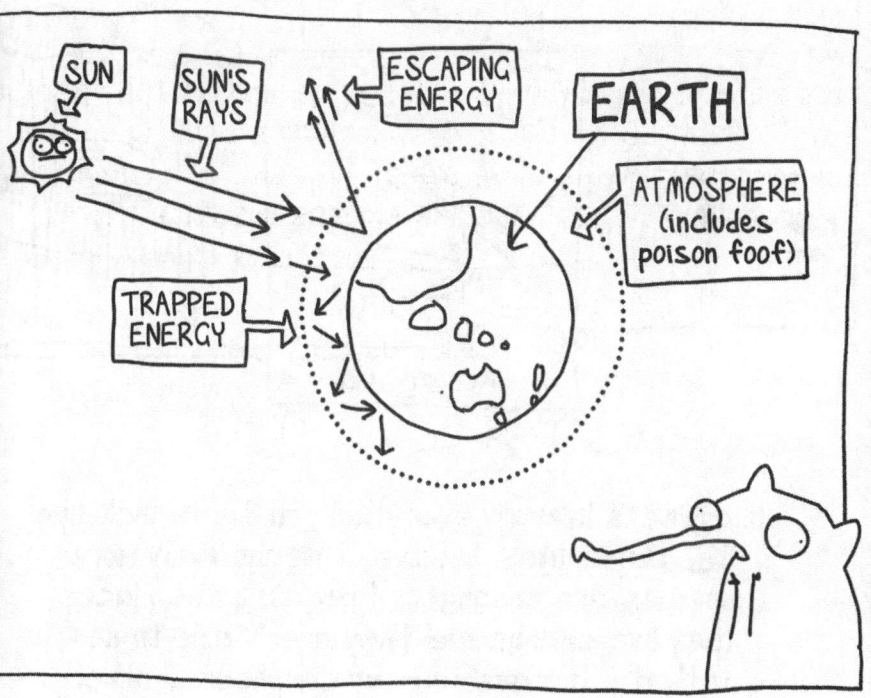

Heat from the sun that would normally leave the atmosphere now stays. An increase of just 1 degree doesn't sound like much, but scientists say that it only needs to go up 2 or so degrees to be a disaster.

Remember, climate and weather are two different things. Changing the whole Earth's climate even just a bit affects the weather all over the planet. Things like hotter summers and colder winters, drier droughts, wetter floods, bigger storms that ruin beaches, and it even has the oceans rising and warming because all the ice is melting at the North and South Poles.

It affects literally everything on Earth including the way animals behave. It means many more species are endangered because the places they live change and they aren't able to deal with it — it leads to many complicated other problems which are right now threatening the whole Earth. It really sucks.

Listen. There are lots of different people contributing to climate change in many different ways. But 70% of it comes from just 100 companies. And the more wealth a country has the more they make climate change worse — either by doing it at home in their country or by paying money to poorer countries to make climate change worse over there wherever it is.

Also deforestation is a huge problem for climate change and anyone who needs trees (everyone).

We can fix some of climate change if we use renewable energy like wind and sun instead of fossil fuels. We can't put everything back the way it was but we can slow it down and even stop it from getting worse. Scientists know everything we need to know. Humans can look after the Earth if enough of them want to.

We don't have to live this way but this is the way we are living right now.

So you're saying adult humans have known this has been happening for years and years

Yes

They know there are better, cleaner ways to live on the Earth without ruining it

Yes

And yet they are not doing it

Yes

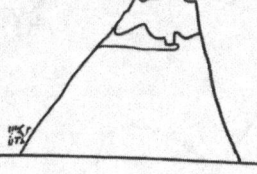

Binky runs off and everyone follows. Back down the slippery volcano, through the poison armpit forest, across the raging river and the hippity hoppity lake of lava.

*(It's in the glossary)

✏ SENGI SCIENCE MOMENT! ✏

Elephant shrews, also called sengis, are small insectivorous mammals from Africa. They got the name "elephant shrew" because their long nose looks like the trunk of an elephant but they ALSO look like shrews. ADORABLE! However (and this is hilarious), phylogenetic analysis shows that elephant shrews are not real shrews, but are in fact more closely related to elephants.

They are a sort of TINY ELEPHANT! 🐘

I mean not really

BUT SORT OF! No theyre not.

Phylogenetics is the study of how some very different species evolved from similar sorts of animals. They're kind of family. Like humans and chimpanzees, that sort of thing.

3 metres | ELEPHANT — 25cm | ELEPHANT SHREW — 5cm | SHREW

Elephants, sengis, dugongs, whales and alpacallamas (not shrews) are all kinds of ungulates. They all evolved from the same kinds of animals over millions of years into the very different creatures we know today. Some of them were probably turned into fossil fuels after they died. That is so weird and I didn't even make it up! There is some more information about shrews in the glossary.

Chapter 10 (Ten)

HOW TO PUT MASCARA ON A WOBBEGONG

In which Binky and her friend Stuart the wobbegong try out some new mascara and launch a petition to put an end to climate change.

Remember the petition we did that time they were going to close the kitten hospital and put all those sick kittens to work at the mousetrap factory!? We got that turned around, so why not this?

At the same time we are going to fundraise a bunch of awareness raising money to raise climate change awareness!

Anyway so climate change is really bad right Stuart?

Typical Monotreme Extreme viewer (could be you!)

Hi everyone, welcome to The Monotreme Extreme Show! Today we'll be putting make-up on our new friend Stuart the wobbegong who we rescued from the aquarium.

Hi Stuart

We're going to do cat's eye eyeliner on someone who spends most of their time under water - we'll be using Slinky Gwendolyn's Super Duper Water-repellent Lash-plumpening Burst Blast with Collagen-thickening Liquid Pillow Wand! It's wild!

And then later on Stuart's favourite segment —
Things to Know in an Emergency. We will be showing you how to escape if you are tied up in an airless low-gravity environment and why you should ALWAYS have a "travel-size spacesuit" in your EDC (every day carry) wherever you go because you just don't know do you.

But first I want to remind everyone about the petition we have put on WHATAREYOUPEOPLEEVENDOING.COM You should all sign and tell your friends and family and pets because it is about climate change which if you haven't heard is literally quite possibly going to cause the end of civilisation I'm not even joking.

YOU SIGNING THE PETITION

GOOD JOB!

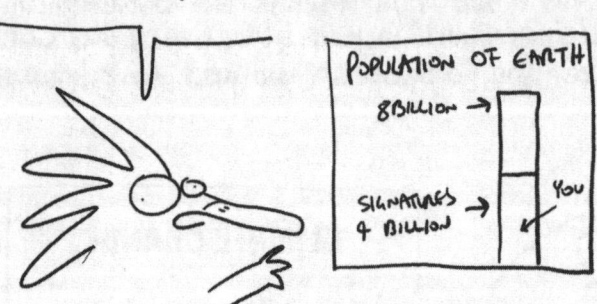

And I know not everyone has money but this week's worthy cause is a super important one it's...

Climate change awareness raising! We are raising money for our good friends the pomeranians at Climate Change Awareness Raising Pomeranians Raising Awareness of Climate Change

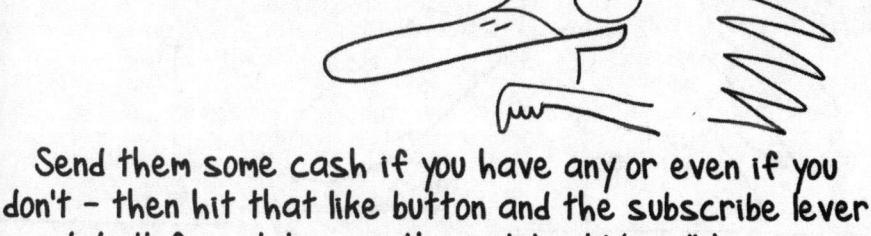

Send them some cash if you have any or even if you don't - then hit that like button and the subscribe lever and don't forget to sign the petition! We will know in a couple of days if we have solved climate change

Climate Change Awareness Raising Pomeranians Raising Awareness of Climate Change Pomeranianly

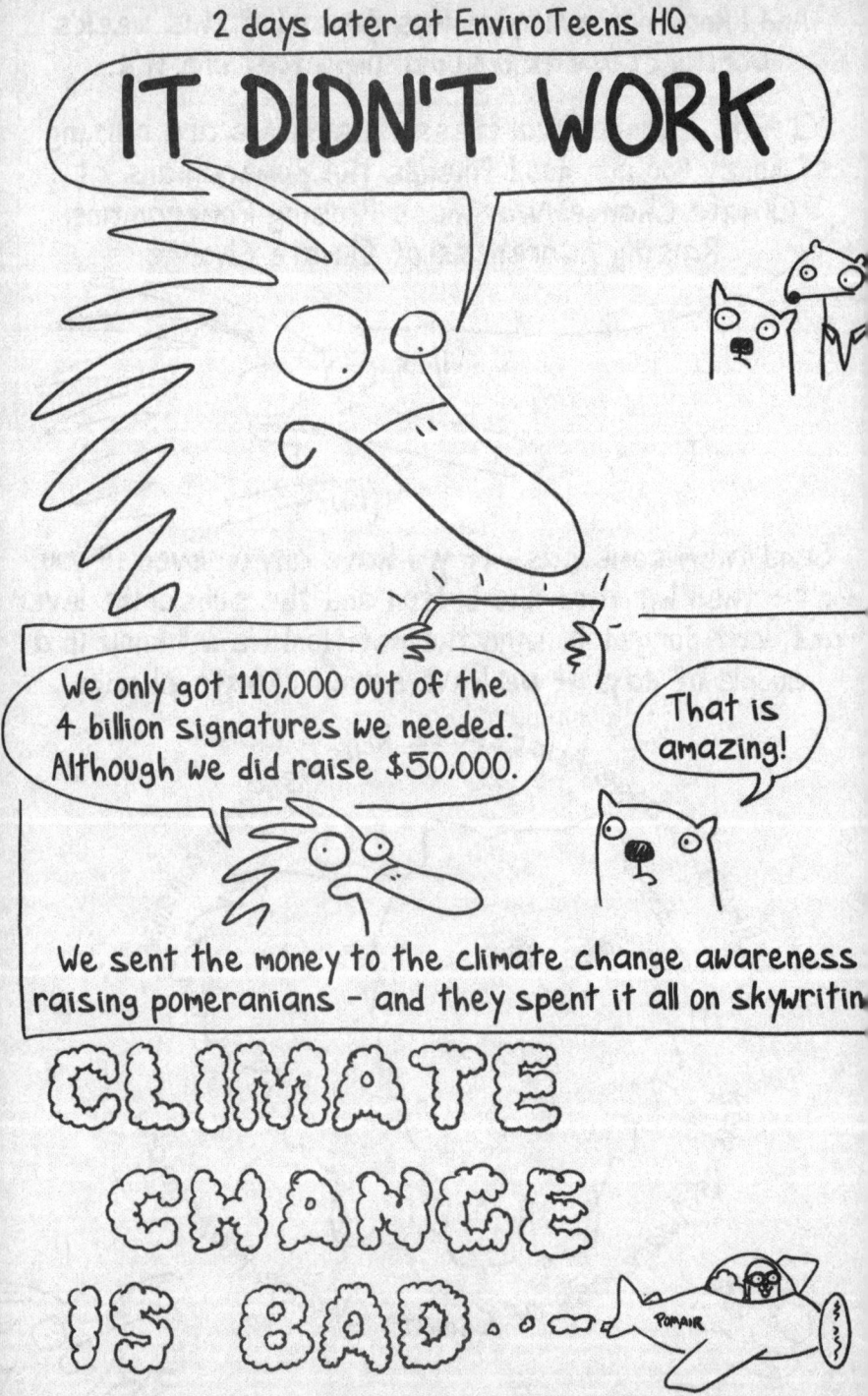

Meanwhile, across the city at the very top of a fancy gilded office tower a meeting is taking place. Who are these terrible people what is going on?

"I've told you all before – just stick to the plan and we will be fine."

"But boss, the EnviroTeens turned Singleuse Plastic Brendan into a BUTTER DISH!"

"You fools! We will do to these so-called EnviroTeens what we have done with every environmental cause, organisation, political party or good idea we have ever encountered – we will squish them with money and power and making things up about them!"

"What even is a butter dish?"

End of meeting! Hands on wallets as we sing the Institute song!

The Sinister Fossil Fuel Institute Anthem*

> We pretend that climate change
> is just a passing fad
>
> When climate change then happens
> we pretend it's not that bad
>
> Then when it's bad we say that
> it will cost too much to fix
> and it's too late to do anything about it
>
> Chorus! Everybody sing
>
> Climate change just isn't happening
> It's a made-up pseudo science thing
> We just want to keep on maaaaaking cash
> and pumping poison foof into the sky
>
> POISON FOOF OI!

* To the tune of the Battle Hymn of the Republic (or Little Peter Rabbit)

Chapter 11

BEVERLY AND THE COMPOST HEAP OF TREACHERY

In which Norman goes home to change his socks and have some feelings and we learn about the mysterious and ancient martial art of bain-marie.

Anyway I know you're anxious but there's no use worrying about things you can't control is there.

I'm serious about that. You can only do the best you can do.

She does have a point there...

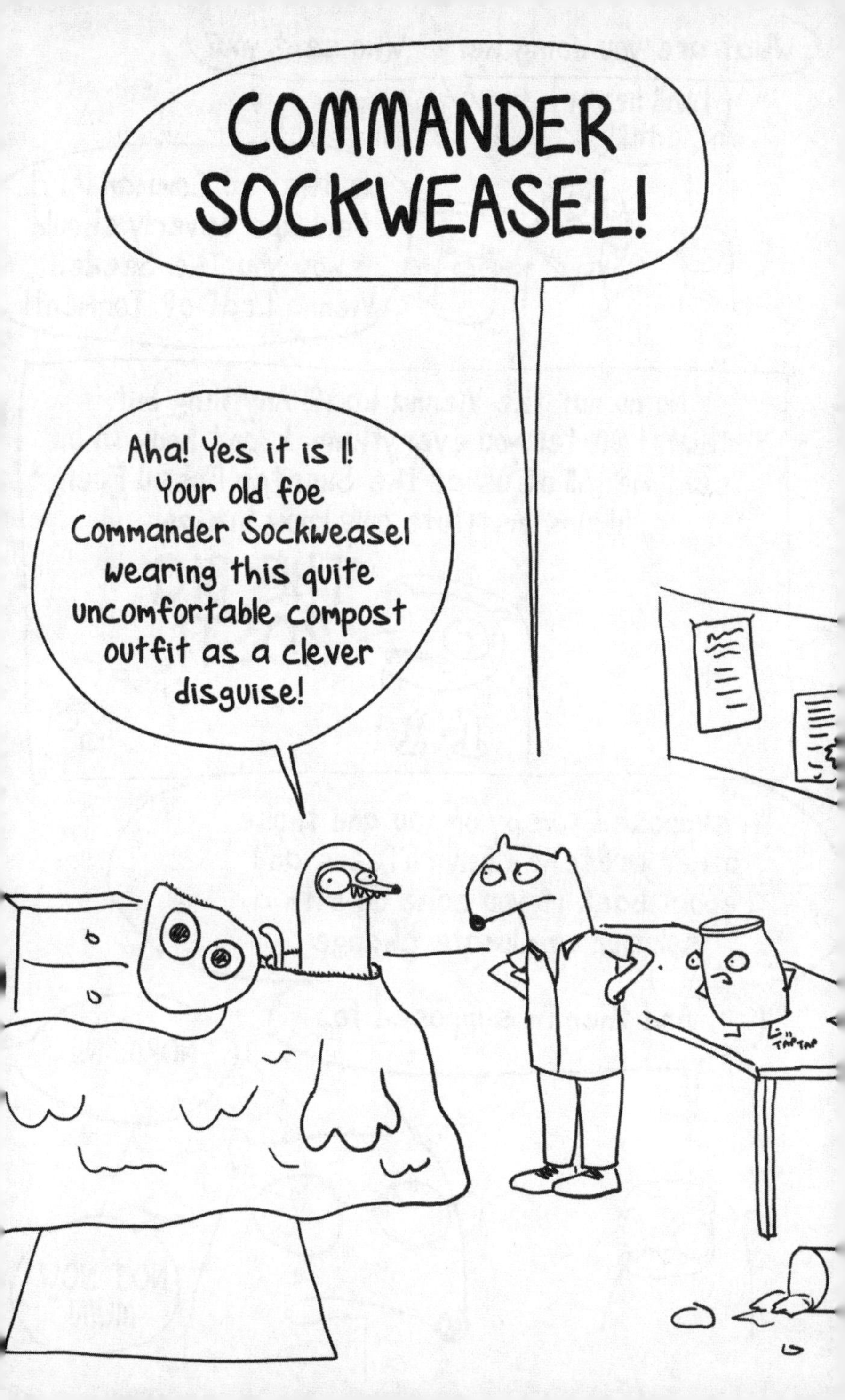

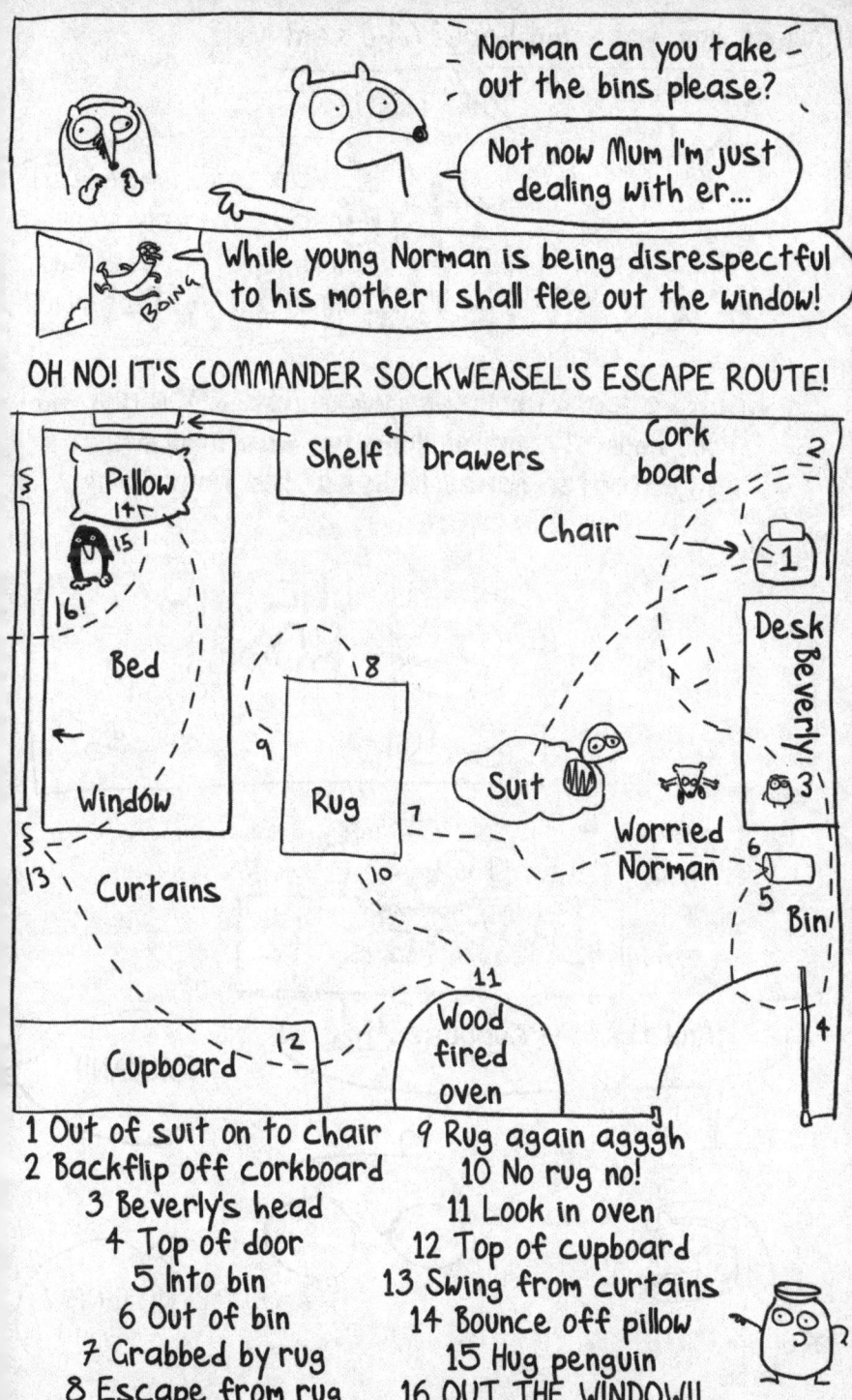

CHAPTER 12

THE EXCITING PLAN

In which we learn about writing on THE MOON and did you know the Prime Minister has a giant anteater named Melissa? It's true!

The planet is being ruined so wealthy adults can have a second jet ski

I don't know whether to be scared or sad or angry or something else

I just want to biff them all

Yeah!

"We are gonna build a LLAMA!?"

"Actually it was an alpaca however..."

"What we need is something that all the adults won't be able to ignore or just shop away like they do their other "problems"."

"Not just a rally or whatever because at the end everyone goes home. But what if everyone does something like...."

Chapter Thirteen is entitled

Hello Potato

Also known as "The mystery of the stolen stollen"

In which we meet an important government root vegetable and there is a terrible biscuit misunderstanding.

Binky and Stuart are on FaceTuba

"Hi everyone – today I'm gonna tell you our plan to save the world and how you can help. It's easy! All you have to do is completely ignore your parents and any other adults in your life. It won't really seem any different from normal."

"Make sure you like and subscribe!"

Letitia is working with the bandicoots to build a prototype defoofiliser

And Norman...

"Come on Beverly we're going to the Moon! But first, the French patisserie!"

The plan is a huge success.

The first defoofiliser is built and it works! Plans are underway to build some more and put them all around the world to start defoofilising. Children everywhere simply ignore bedtime and refuse to clean their rooms. It is chaos!

"No Mother I shan't eat another morsel of kale until you show me your realistic implementation schedule for nationwide Utility-Scale Solar Photovoltaics.*"

*That is a network of solar panel "farms" so big it could power whole cities.

Meanwhile, using tonnes of abandoned baking equipment and radioactive pierogis from the Chernobyl reactor, Pastry Person was able to write a message on the Moon. The Moon is a long way away so it had to be huge — we asked some Moon-writing scientists who said the writing needed to be about 500,000 square kilometres (the size of a single France)

So not as big as the Pacific Garbage Patch (3 Frances) but still very big.

Stop climate change!

Hello hello these must be the marvellous EnviroTeens! It really is a profound honour to meet such a plucky crew of inspirational young people — you've certainly gotten everyone's attention with your bold and er... unorthodox strategy to battle the scourge of "climate change" as you call it

But of course how rude am I neglecting to introduce myself! I am the Minister for the Environment, Senator Ian the Climate Denialist Potato.

Call me Ian

...and of course you are Letitia – the scientific wombat genius – I'd know those powerful claws anywhere.

Enchanté mademoiselle, I have heard so much about your cunning defoofiliser.

You know you mustn't let these others hold you back, you could be a world-famous scientist one day

And this must be the magnificent Pastry Person! The Moon-writing fellow himself. Goodness what a captivating lunar spectacle it all is –

Pity about the typo

The what?

The defoofiliser's solar-powered vacuumatic slurpivalve sucks up all the nearby poison foof and flunges it through the hypermagnetronic resnoffelling filter to remove all of the carbules. Then it is passed at light speed down the anti-gravitational spoo-duct to be fnogulised by a back-ended homulising frant-array that spits the remains out the plamping chute into a bucket. All that's left behind is a few nuggets of Niffleonium - and you won't believe this - all the bandicoots at the workshop thought this was hilarious because - Niffleonium is a previously unknown form of completely renewable energy that is hugely powerful and totally clean - oh how we laughed and laughed.

We got such a shock. Almost burnt my eyebrows off.

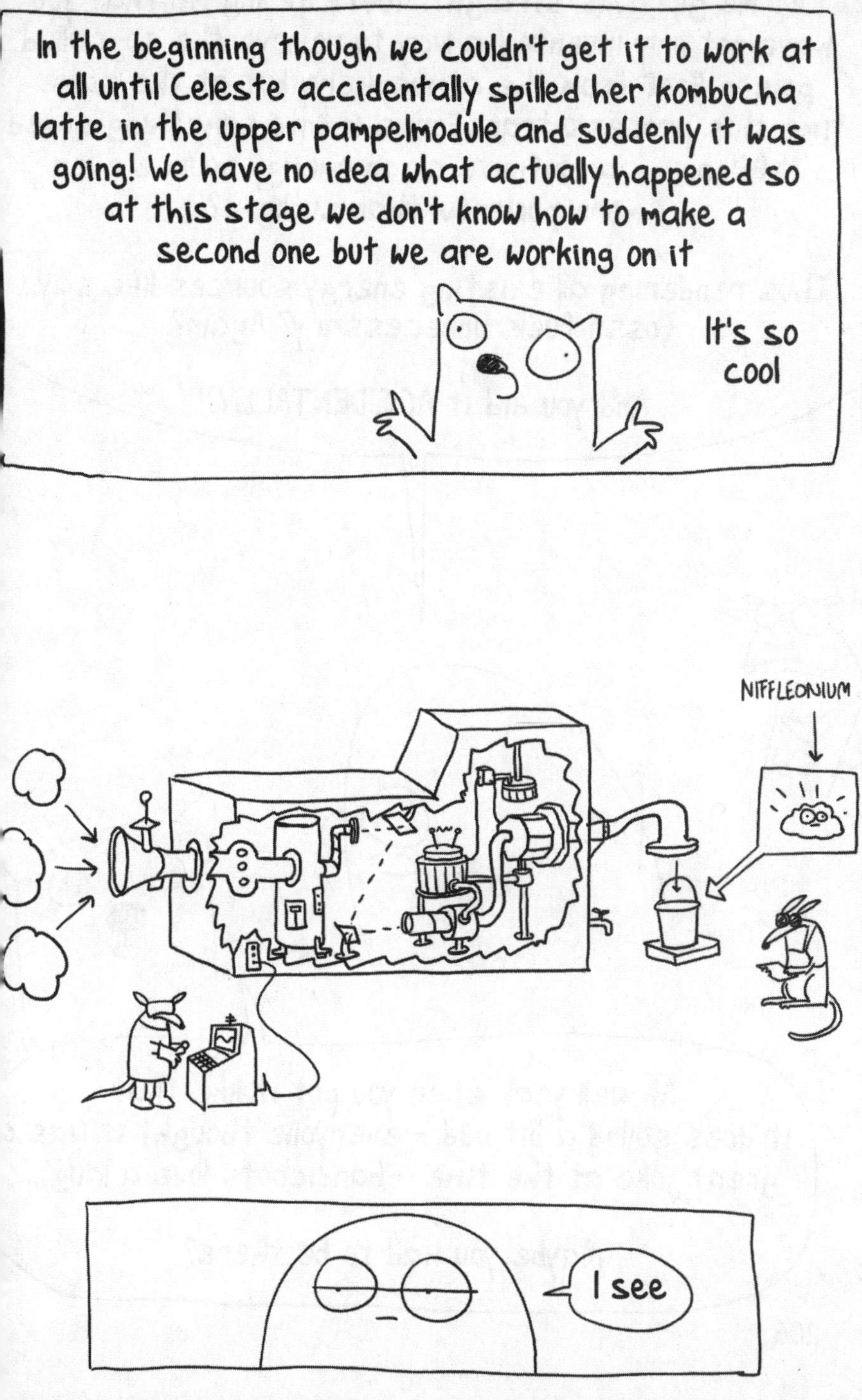

In the beginning though we couldn't get it to work at all until Celeste accidentally spilled her kombucha latte in the upper pampelmodule and suddenly it was going! We have no idea what actually happened so at this stage we don't know how to make a second one but we are working on it

It's so cool

NIFFLEONIUM

I see

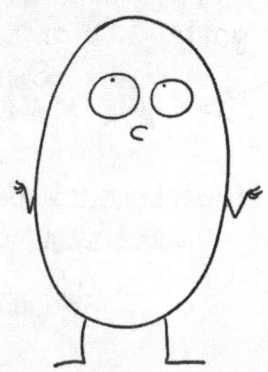

Well I don't know anything about that perhaps they are attracted to err... kombucha lattes? Who knows!

You'll have to excuse us minister but we need to take the defoofiliser back to the workshop and find out what happened

Of course children of course! It was lovely to meet you – we are very proud of all the work you've done saving the world and if there's ever anything I or this Doing Things Government can do for you, you let me know

Byeee

To the EnviroHonk!

Chapter 14

A FALLING OUT

In which things start to get weird and shouty. But I'm sure it will be ok.

OR WILL IT?! I DON'T KNOW?!

HELP!

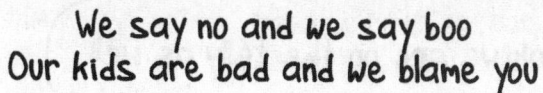

I courageously confronted these alleged "ecoyouths" about their dangerous defoofilising machine and how it had injured the Prime Minister's giant anteater they all laughed and said mean things

These juveniles are an uncouth rabble! They are out of control and encouraging many impressionable children to wildly disrespect authority all because of climate change which many sensible people say isn't even real

and they can't even spell it properly

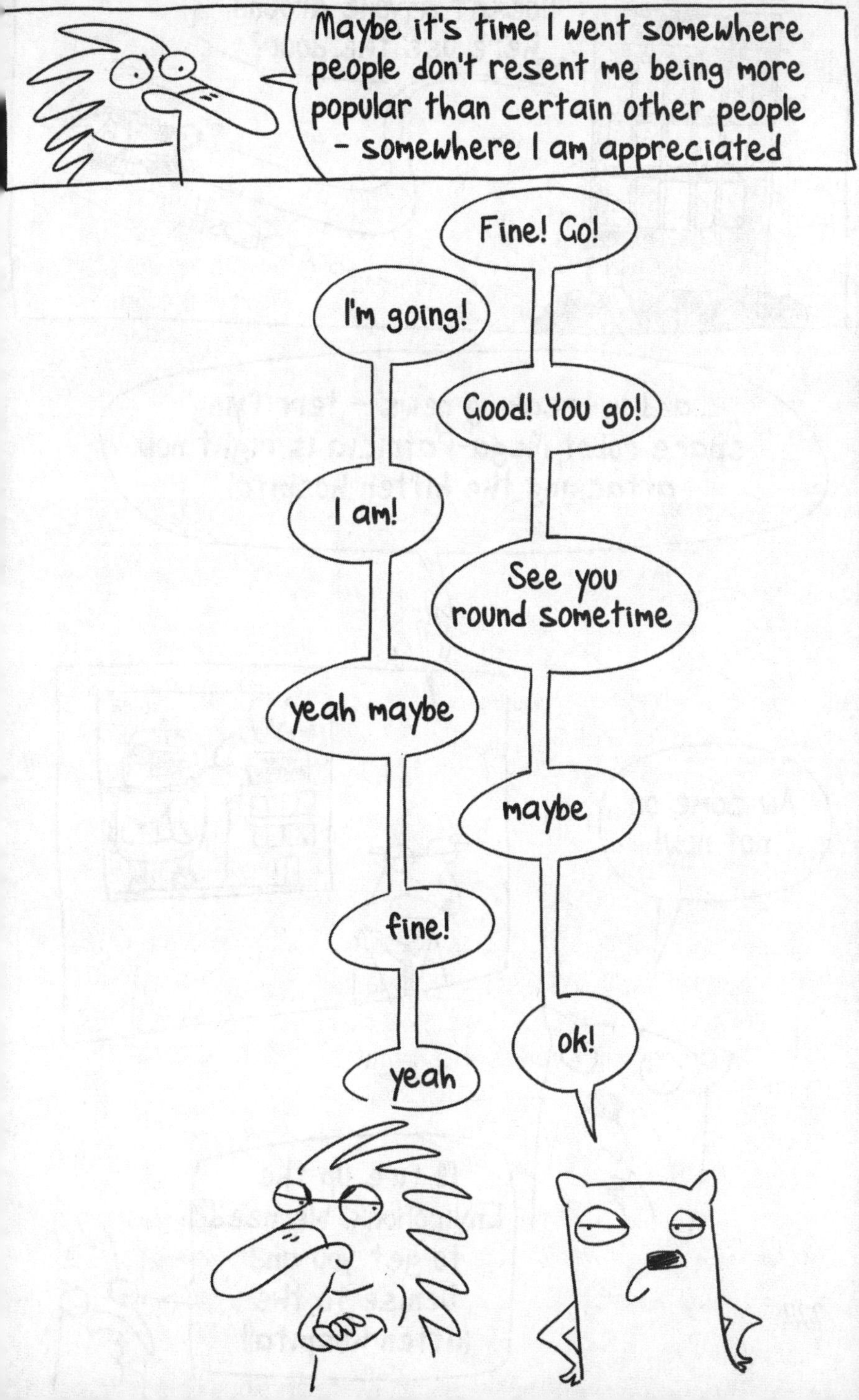

Chapter 15
~~THE FIENDISH ATTACK ON THE BANDICOOT WORKSHOP~~
Chapter 3 makes a cup of tea

In which Chapter 3 asks nicely if Chapter 15 might squooge over just a bit so it can have a go as it missed out when everyone was so busy between Chapter 2 and Chapter 4

"What is this? What are you doing? Where is Chapter 15?"

"We are just going to have a nice cup of tea and hold our signs for a bit"

"But I have to save the world!"

"The whole thing? That sounds exhausting!"

"I'm sorry! ok! I'm just trying to get everything done!"

"And I'm sorry about not telling you about the Moon spelling I wasn't laughing at you and I'm sorry I made the scones cry"

"And Chapter 3"

"And Chapter 3"

"Hey sorry about the Moon thing bread face"

"No worries — I know you didn't mean it"

"Without me telling everyone what to do can we go SAVE THE DEFOOFILISER NOW?!"

Chapter 47

"Save the Defooflethingy or whatever it is"

"What now?"

"Hi I'm Sandra from the Chapter employment agency. They said you needed someone to fill in. Sorry for any confusion – I usually do the glossary."

"Hi Sandra can we just get on with it please?"

"Sure – here you go"

CHAPTER Hello

"It is time to show these hugely annoying villains what a Monotreme can do!"

Binky becomes a blur of interclavicle fury! With a super-powerful shoulder charge she crunches the entire Sinister Fossil Fuel Institute and they all land on their villainous bottoms... ahahaha I said bottoms

SMACKITYPOW!

CLANG!

FLAP FLAP

AAAGH!

Wait a blur of interclaviwhat now?

Tiny Science Moment! – Did you know Monotremes have super bones in their shoulders? True! Echidnas and platypuses have extra "interclavicle" and "coracoid" bones which are not found in other mammals. Because Binky is a platypus AND an echidna she has double extra, thus giving her quadruple the amount of shoulder power than anyone else ON EARTH.

SUPER SHOULDER

OTHER SUPER SHOULDER

It looks like Binky has saved the day. OR HAS SHE?!

Suddenly there is a streak of beige fire...

Oh yeah it's Beverly!

Beverly!

You've saved the day! Shouldn't you be at home protecting the house from compost heaps?

We're so glad you made it

BY THE POWER OF GLUUUUUTENNNN!!

AAAAAAAAAKKZZZ

Chapter 16

DENOUEMENT ON THE MOON

In which the EnviroTeens are betrayed and thrust into grim danger! Will they survive? Where is the defoofiliser? Oh dear.

It's almost the end of the book! It's so exciting I can't bear it!

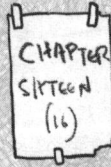

And crash they do! Thank goodness everyone is ok. Except the EnviroHonk which is wrecked. Fortunately Norman can become Pastry Person who can fly back to Earth and.....

"Melissa what are you doing?"

"She's taken all of Norman's croissants! How will we get back to Earth if he can't become Pastry Person!?"

"Where is she going?"

"Maybe it's the Big Rosti's secret Moon base!"

SECRET MOON BASE

GO AWAY

Pastry Person has been coming up here every day for months to change the Stop Climate Chonge sign. I never saw any of this. It is so secret!

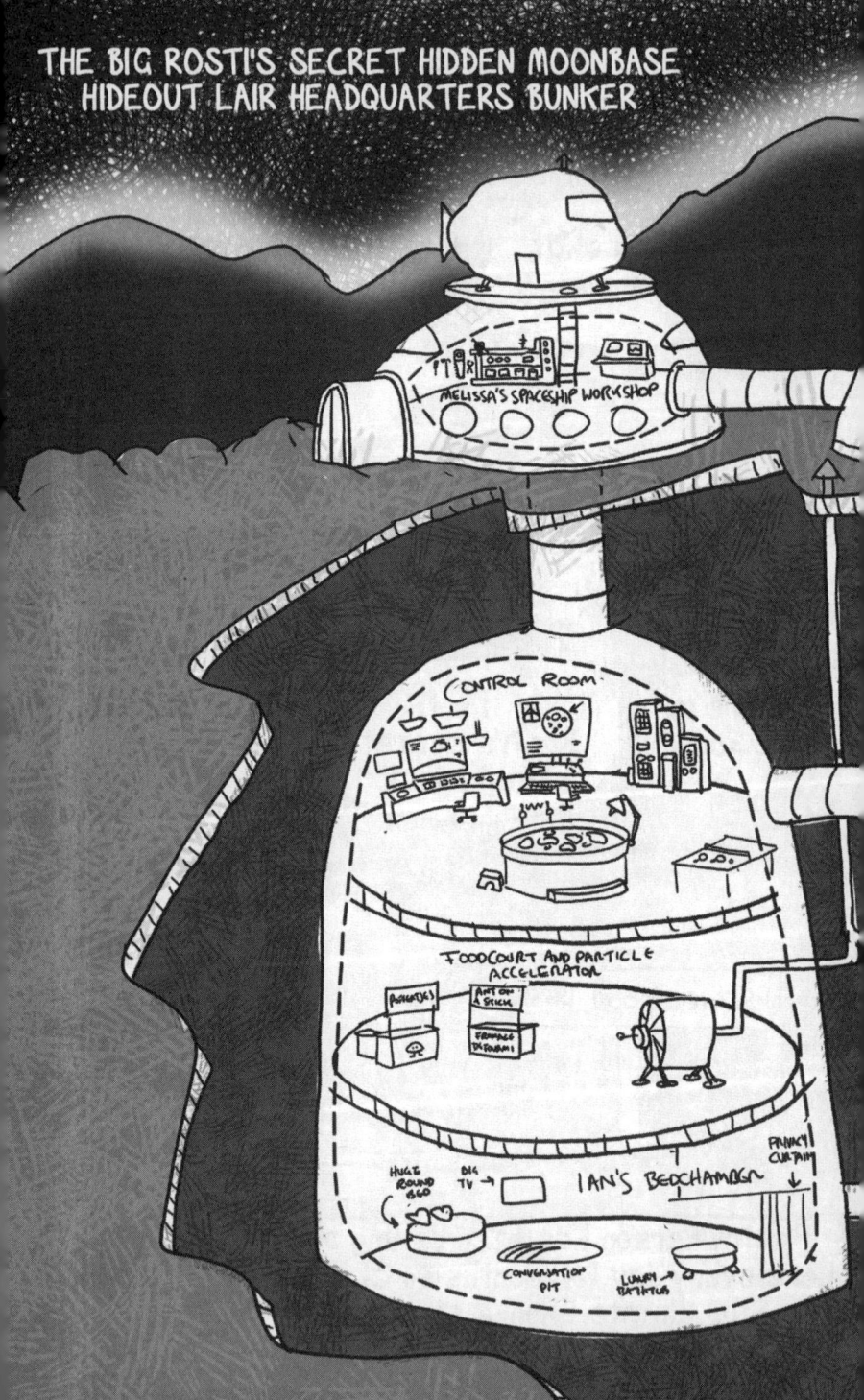

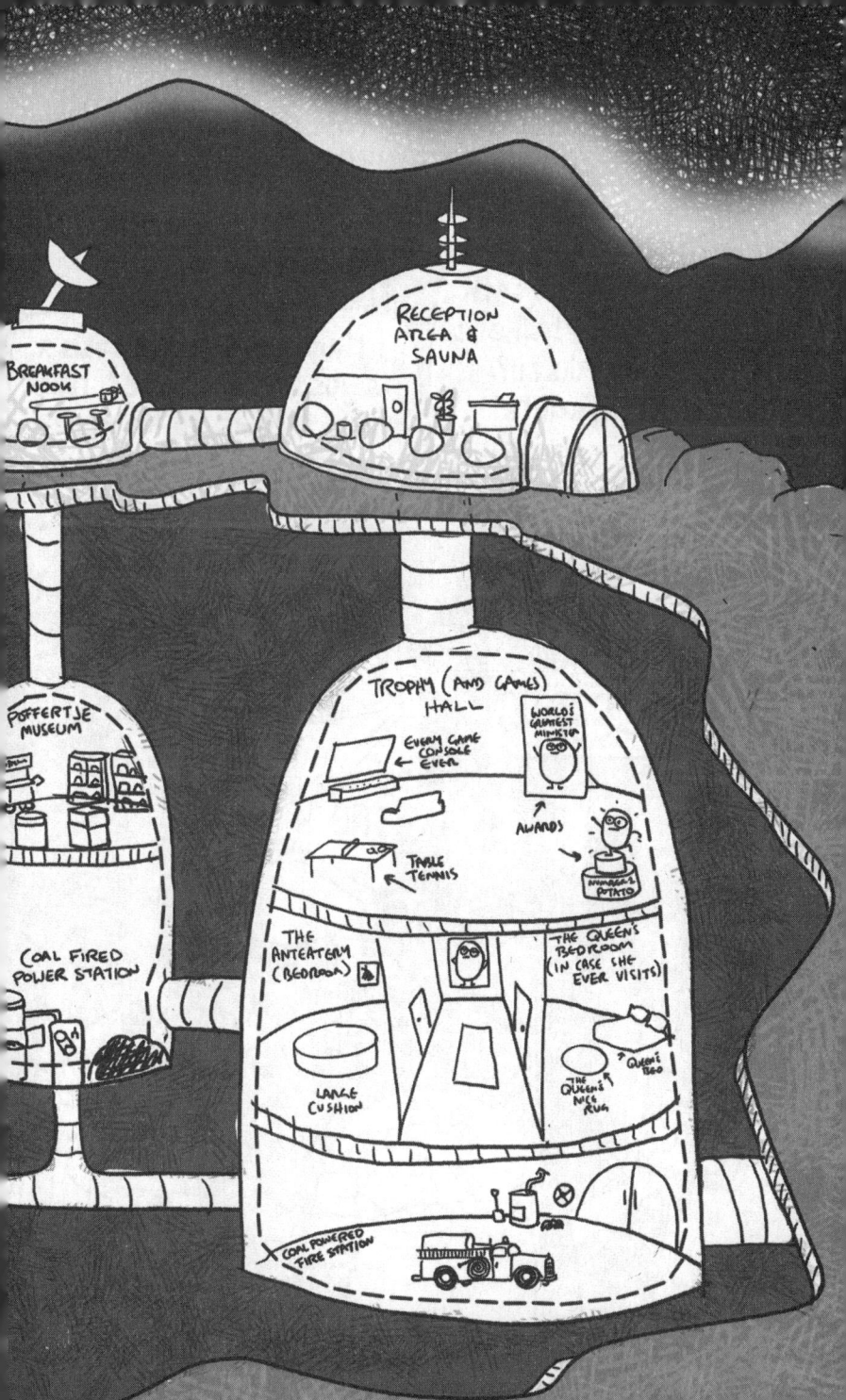

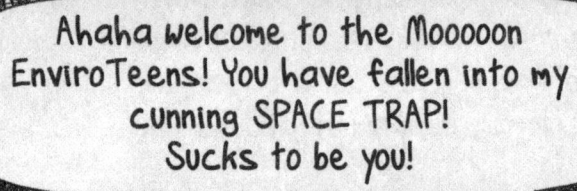

That's right! Melissa has been working for me the whole time — she is normally employed in my electorate office as a paper shredder and generally helps out around the place.

It was Melissa who planted the ant cheese in the defoofiliser and then got her nose caught although that part was an accident but it all worked out perfectly!

She stole your spacebrakes AND your croissants...

You heard me EnviroSooks don't come any closer or the wobbegong gets it! You all get it! Don't make me push this "explode the Moon" button on my exploding the Moon remote control.

But that will blow up you too!

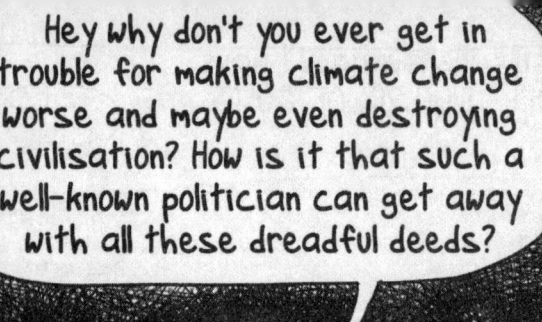

Aboard the space potato.

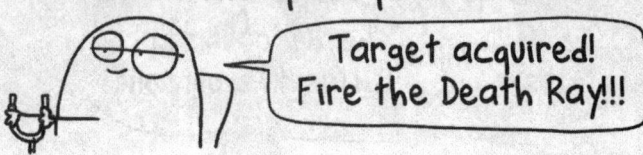

Target acquired! Fire the Death Ray!!!

All of a sudden there is a bolt of taupe lightning...

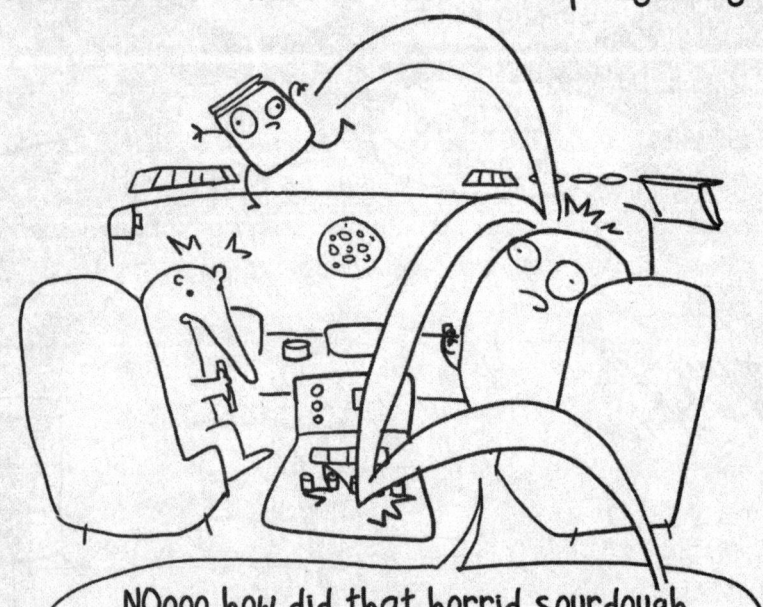

NOooo how did that horrid sourdough starter get in here! Keep it away from the hot chip death ray!

Beverly springs on Melissa's head just as the giant anteater shoots the enormous ray gun. The ray gun misses the huge pile of Moon explosives however....

KRAKAZAKKLE CRICKLE FRIZZ
DEEPFRY NOISES BZZZT HONK DING

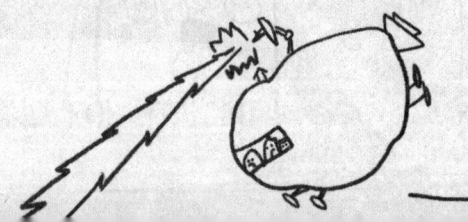

"You wretched artisanal bucket of flour! Prepare to be deep-fried!"

crackfrackle

The Big Rosti shoots Beverly with his TGI Fry Ray but he misses and the beam hits....

ACTIVATE AUTOPILOT ONE WAY TRIP TO MARS WITH NO WAY TO TURN THE SPACESHIP AROUND AT ALL

DO NOT PRESS THIS BUTTON!

BOING! *click!*

uh o

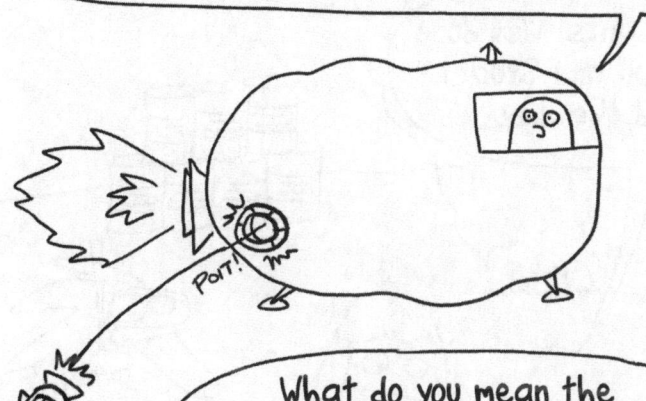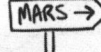

Chapter The End

In which the EnviroTeens return everything that was stolen to Nifflenose Island also oh my goodness all that Moon business was so exciting my bottom caught on fire I had to go and sit in the bath!

and er... where is Captain Snoothole anyway?

I'm Captain Snoothole every Tuesday and every second Sunday - we take turns "running" the refuge - makes it much easier if visitors think someone is in charge. People get uncomfortable if they can't figure out who the boss is (it's all of us, well... more like none of us)

Last time you were here Flippitypingpong was Captain Snoothole. She's off helping build an extension to the Walrusry - they're adding an underwater pool room!

TURTLE LAYING AREA THIS WAY

OR THAT WAY

OR WHEREVER WORKS FOR YOU

the end

end

OR IS IT!?

SORT OF

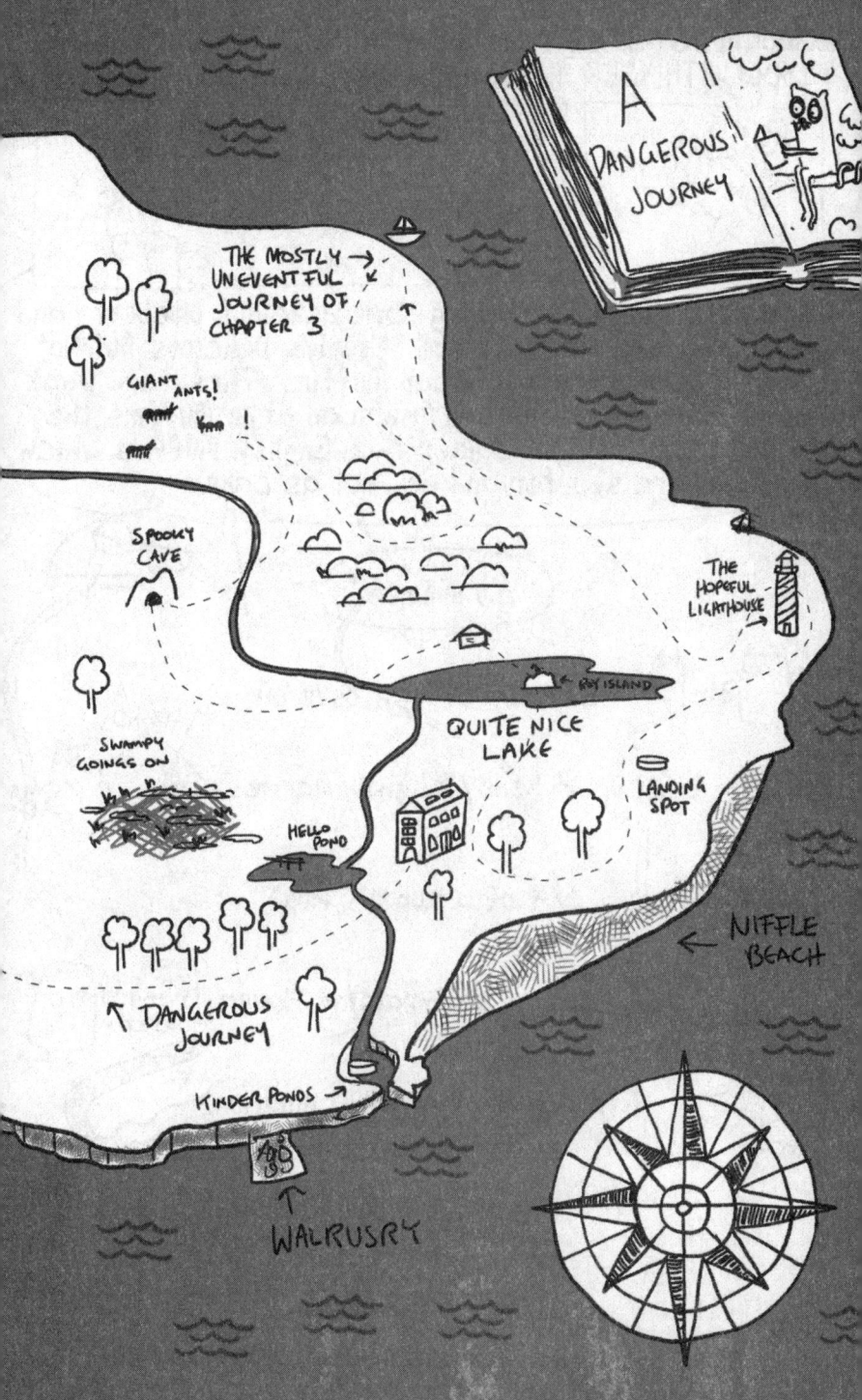

OH MY CHEESY BISCUITS IT'S EVERYONE'S FAVOURITE BAKING SHOW WITH YOUR HOSTS PASTRY PERSON AND BEVERLY

Hi bakers! Today we're baking some delicious blueberry and pecan muffins which we call Beverly's Delicious But Not Sourdough Blueberry and Pecan Muffins. These are what we in the baking scene call American Style Muffins they are taller and sort of cakier than English Muffins which are shorter and er... not as cakey.

You will need:

 1/4 cup of light olive oil

1/2 cup of honey (slightly warmed)

 3/4 of a cup of "milk"

2 cups of self-raising flower

1 teaspoon of ground cinnamon

1/2 cup of chopped pecans

 1 cup of blueberries

The EnviroTeen Plan To Defeat Climate Change and Save the World MANIFESTO

1. The poison foofing has to stop. It won't stop by itself so the system that keeps it going has to change. That is what we will do. No more wrecking the planet.

2. We are building a world that is nicer and safer, where being selfish and cruel is a character flaw not a sign that someone should be in charge of anything.

3. Everyone gets to have somewhere clean and safe to live, free health care and school and enough food and clean water I mean some people don't even have clean water that is ridiculous

4. Nobody anywhere should have a single cent more than the poorest person on earth

5. We will join with other young people to freak out, strike, agitate, discombombulate and change the world. Community is the way to do all this.

6. We will not take no for an answer. There is no no. To no, we say no.

7. All the land will be returned to the people it was stolen from. All of it.

8. Hope is a feeling, it is not a plan. We need both.

9. We should all do more baking.

If you want to know more or do more, check out these websites

www.schoolstrike4climate.com
www.seedmob.org.au

Hi everyone I'm Sandra and I'm here to help with the GLOSSARY.

Boules – a larger hard ball used in pétanque (see pétanque)

Capitalism – an economic system where a country's businesses and profits are controlled by private companies owned by a small group of wealthy people, and not by the other much larger group of people who do all of the actual work for those companies. It is not a fair way of sharing the world's limited resources or taking care of everyone. It is also destroying the planet.

Carbon Neutral – when something does NOT produce carbon or anything else that contributes to climate change. Although sometimes businesses and governments use the phrase to pretend they are not making climate change worse. For example, someone chops down an old forest somewhere and then plants a few trees somewhere else. Then they say "we fixed it we are carbon neutral". But it's not the same.

Cochonnet – a small ball you have to get your boules near during pétanque (see pétanque)

Denouement – a French word which means the end bit of the story where it all comes together.

Glossary – this is one. It is an explainy list of unexpected words such as you might find at the back of a book.

Indefatigable – tireless and enthusiastic. Yeah! Never give up! Go! Woohoooo! Make it happen like a chicken!

Keratin – a fibrous protein that is the main part of growing things like hair, feathers, rhino horn, turtle shells, your fingernails. ALL MADE OF THE SAME THING HELLO TURTLE FINGERS!

Manifesto – important list which is used to tell other people your plans and things you believe in

Pétanque – a game in which you win by having your boules closer to the cochonnet than your opponent (see boules and also cochonnet)

Poison Foof – not actually poisonous but things like carbon dioxide (CO_2) and methane (CH_4) and their friends are greenhouse gases. They are the main contributors to climate change – don't forget that plants love carbon dioxide and it is harmless in small quantities. It is called poison foof in this book because is a funny thing to say.

Sengi – not a shrew but looks like one (see shrew)

Sentient – something that can perceive or feel things

Shrew – tiny wee beastie with a wiffly nose – eats bugs and lives in the forest – related to moles and hedgehogs

Sourdough starter – a mixture of yeast and water and flour which becomes sentient and wants to take over the world also you can make sourdough bread from it

Acknowledgements and freshly
baked thank youse to

Scott Ludlam, Ketan Joshi, Sophie Black, Anthony Morgan, Sue Plant, Jon Kudelka, Calla Wahlquist, Lisa Cox, Adam Morton, Graham Readfearn, Lenore Taylor, Kath Viner, Nicola Paris, Svetlana Stankovic, Jo Tovey, Boyd O'Donnell, Roy the border collie, all the chickens (Purple, Maybelle, June, Loretta, Tammy), David Paris, all the sheep (Gently, Adele, Noodle), Anna McFarlane, Nicola Santilli (who appears in this book), Liz Seymour, Jane Novak (my agent), Michael Williams, Ruby Krupka, everyone at Chicken Club, Marcus Bontempelli and everyone involved in the 2016 AFL Grand Final, Bridie Jabour, SS4C and most of all to Marieke Hardy.

And also even more most of all to Bronte Saurus

A special wombat hello and you're welcome to the crew of extremely helpful bandicoots in the EnviroTeens bookwriting factory workshop

Ashar, Bella, Clementine, Harper, Hedley, Henry, Maggie, Oskar and Walt

JOIN US FOR THE NEXT EXCITING INSTALLMENT

RETURN TO NIFFLENOSE ISLAND!

or maybe

ALIEN POTATO ARMY FROM MARS

or even

AROUND THE WORLD
IN 80 LAUNDRY BASKETS
The further adventures of Beverly

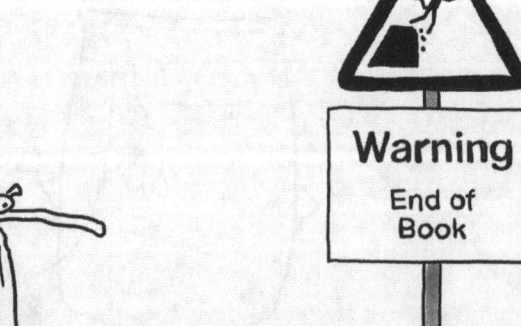